DOUBLED IN DIAMONDS

Victor Canning's first novel, *Mr Finchley Discovers His England*, was published in 1934, since which time he has been a full-time author. He now has over thirty novels to his credit, of which *The Great Affair* is the latest. He is also the author of many short stories and serials which have been published in the principal newspapers and magazines of England and America.

Born in Plymouth in 1911, Victor Canning was a features writer for the *Daily Mail* before the Second World War, during which he was commissioned in the Royal Artillery. He has worked as a scriptwriter in Hollywood and now lives in Kent.

His recent novels include *Doubled in Diamonds*, *The Python Project*, *The Melting Man* and *Queen's Pawn*.

DOUBLED IN DIAMONDS

VICTOR CANNING

UNABRIDGED

PAN BOOKS LTD : LONDON
By arrangement with
WILLIAM HEINEMANN LTD
LONDON

First published 1966 by Wm. Heinemann Ltd.
This edition published 1968 by Pan Books Ltd,
33 Tothill Street, London SW1

ISBN 0 330 02125 7

2nd Printing 1973

© Victor Canning, 1966

Printed in Great Britain by
Cox & Wyman Ltd, London, Reading and Fakenham

ONE

Man Wanted

SLEET-LADEN wind blew up from the river and, now and again, there was a pea-shot rattle of hail against the window. Bracing stuff – so long as you were comfortably inside with the central heating turned up full blast.

I slewed my chair round, bored with the Northumberland Avenue traffic, and stared at a naked girl sitting under a palm tree on the wall calendar.

The door opened and Hilda Wilkins came in. She had a folded newspaper in her hand and she said, 'Good morning' in a voice thick with a cold. Her nose was almost as red as her hair and her blue eyes were misty with Benzedrex tears.

I said, 'Why don't you go home, wrap an old sock round your neck and get into bed? Your father can take time off from studying form and coddle you with onion soup.'

She sniffed and dropped the paper in front of me, still folded. I could see that it was *The Times* – a paper I seldom read.

She said, 'Are you going to sit there all day, doing nothing?'

'Why not?' I'd already put in two months' practice.

'The bills are piling up. Electricity, rates, and your bank manager—'

'Don't tell me what he said. He's got a one-track mind.'

I picked up the paper and opened it, getting the full spread of the small print of the advertisement page.

'If work doesn't come to you – go out and find it,' Wilkins said.

'You got that off some motto calendar.'

Close to the top of the first personal column a blue

pencil circle had been drawn round an announcement.

'You have,' said Wilkins, 'a very primitive emotional make-up.'

'I've got along with it very well all these years.'

'You only have two emotional states. Apathetic or excited.'

'Which do you prefer?'

'If anything – the latter.'

I said, 'I think I'm beginning to like doing nothing. Apathy suits me. If anything made me excited now I'd probably break up altogether. Why don't you go home to bed and get rid of that cold?'

She said, 'Read that announcement.'

I read it.

FINCH, JESSIE, deceased. – Would Arnold Finch, only surviving relative of the late Jessie Finch, who formerly resided at 31 Nassington Road, Hampstead, London, NW3, please communicate with Armstrong and Pepper, Solicitors, Tewkes Chambers, Chancery Lane, London, WC2, where he will learn of something to his advantage.

'So what?' I asked.

'They've run it for a month, and you could get them to let you take over.'

'For fifty pounds and minimal expenses? And in this weather? No thanks. Give me apathy.'

'You've got an appointment with them in half an hour.'

'What?'

'I've just fixed it. You're to see their Managing Clerk, a Mr Lancing. He's agreed to employ you.'

'Agreed?'

'I talked nicely to him and gave you a good build up.'

'And fixed the fee?'

'I said, fifty pounds and reasonable expenses.'

She moved to the hat stand by the door and began to take down my coat, hat and scarf.

I said, 'I'll need snow boots.'

She came back and fussed me into my coat and said, 'I hate to see you moping around.'

'I can't think why. I always do it quietly.'

I got a taxi from the rank outside and we headed east into the teeth of the blizzard. I knew the driver – he'd driven me before. On the way down he said, 'Caught any good criminals lately, Mr Carver? Any juicy divorce cases?' For some odd reason cab drivers always get fresh with me. Anyway I didn't take divorce cases.

I said, 'Keep your eye on the road – or you won't get your threepenny tip.'

Tewkes Chambers was a rabbit warren, and in one of the inner rooms I finally ferreted out Mr Lancing. He was a dried-up Hottentot of an old man who could probably have been drawing an old age pension while I was still at school. He had a brown wrinkled face, weathered by years of law dust and the steam from lunch-time cafés, and he made pleasant preliminary noises at me. When he sat down behind his desk, he was so small that he almost disappeared.

He said, 'That's a very efficient secretary you've got, Mr Carver. Nice manner. Must bring you a lot of business.'

'I'd be lost without her.'

'Behind every successful man, there's always a good woman.' He wrinkled his face up at me.

I smiled. Any lesser man, I suppose, might have been jealous. The brass plate at the foot of our stairs said, Carver and Wilkins. Not Wilkins and Carver.

'Arnold Finch,' I said.

'Ah, yes. His aunt – a late client of ours, Jessie Finch – has recently died. We've been trying to trace him. He's the only surviving relative. We've gone through the usual routine, advertising and so on, but without success. So when your Miss Wilkins telephoned we felt—'

'Quite. How much is involved?'

'Didn't Miss Wilkins tell you? Fifty pounds plus reasonable—'

'No. I mean how much did Miss Jessie Finch leave?'

7

'Oh yes. A little over six thousand pounds.' He put his hand into his inner coat pocket – at least, below the desk, that was what it looked like – and pulled out a folded length of foolscap. 'All the known details we have are set out there.' He handed it over as though he were giving me the freedom of the City of London. I took it and put it in my pocket.

'Photographs?'

'Only one I'm afraid – except for some schoolboy snaps that were with Miss Finch's effects.'

He juggled below the desk and handed over a photograph to me. It was one of those jobs that street photographers take around Trafalgar Square. I could see the pigeons and part of the façade of the National Gallery in the background.

'How did you get this?'

'His aunt, Miss Finch. It was with her stuff. I knew her well. She told me once that every third Sunday in the month she and her nephew would meet for the afternoon and go to art galleries, concerts and so on. This was taken, I presume, on such an occasion.'

'They were on good terms?'

'Oh, yes. But she didn't often see him. Interesting woman. She painted tiles and ashtrays.'

'Why?'

'To supplement her income. She had a small annuity on which she lived. Never touched capital. So she did this pottery work. That's one of hers—' He pushed the ashtray on his desk to me. 'Gave it to me one Christmas.'

I picked it up. It was a bit surprising. In pink and black wash were two semi-naked goddesses, arms twined round one another's necks and gazing deep into one another's eyes. The right foot of one of them floated in the air a little above the initials J.F.

I said, 'Any reason why he shouldn't have come forward by now? I mean character, record, or anything like that?'

'No. He was a little bit of a rolling stone, but nothing

else. I met him once. Absolutely charming – and a gentleman, of course.'

I didn't say anything. I'd met some very charming
gentlemen in my time.

When I got back to the office, Wilkins was out to lunch.
I went into my room, stopped on the way to the desk and
tore off the palm tree girl from the calendar, although she
still had another day to go. Her successor was a real May
girl, warm and brown, watering a bed of red tulips and
wearing nothing but a straw hat. A nice comfortable girl,
fond of gardening, and dressed properly for it.

I sat down and began to read Lancing's notes on Arnold
Finch and his aunt. Miss Jessie Finch had died at the age
of sixty-five in her Hampstead flat with no relations except
her nephew Arnold Finch. Finch was thirty-three, un-
married, and his last known address had been a hotel in
Dorset Square which he'd left four months before. There
was a lot of junk about his prep school and public school,
then London University where he'd got a degree in
Economics. He had done a four-year stint with Imperial
Chemical Industries after University, then had left them
and the record was blank for a long time. Then came a
two-year period as a joint director of a firm called Polyfold Plastics Limited which he had left three months
ago. After that there was no trace of him.

The photograph I had, showed a tall, slim, good-looking man in a well cut lounge suit, smoking a cigarette, the
smoke of which just edged across his face. But the face
was clear enough, long, well boned, intelligent, and the
mouth firm and pleasant. On the back Lancing had written, Fair hair. Five feet eleven.

At this moment Wilkins came in, walked to the desk
and picked up the photograph.

'Arnold Finch,' I said. 'A gentleman, charming, intelligent, and, for some reason, in no hurry to pick up six
thousand pounds. Most men would hurry for that. Six
thousand – and I'm going to slog after him for fifty
quid!'

9

'We need it.'

'Of course. Anyway, you pack up and get home – and don't come back until you've got a clean bill of health.'

'I shall be here tomorrow.'

I didn't argue. I seldom did with Wilkins. She was thirty-five, lived at 20 Circus Street, Greenwich, with her father, a retired ship's steward. Her figure looked as though it had been made with building blocks. She had a heart of gold, an incredible loyalty to me professionally and thought nothing of my morals and manners.

After she had gone I sat there thinking. Arnold Finch was reasonably fond of his aunt. He took her once a month to art galleries. Keeping in with the old girl. Now she was dead – and there was six thousand for him to pick up. A man had to have a good reason for missing that bonus. Or did he? Perhaps the word 'good' was wrong. Well, it was something to bear in mind.

I put on my heavy overcoat, walked around the corner to the pub for a large whisky, was nobbled by a bar stranger who wanted to prove to me that there was no economic future for the country until we had a large pool of unemployed, and then left deciding to try Polyfold Plastics. But I walked first of all down to Miggs's. Behind his garage Miggs had a small gymnasium. It was a couple of guineas a half-hour session – but a lot of people went. Miggs had been a sergeant in the Commandos and was showing a Cabinet Minister how to throw an Opposition member over his right shoulder. When he had finished, Miggs came up to me smelling of Sloan's Liniment, his boiled beetroot face lacquered with sweat.

I said, 'Arnold Finch – mean anything to you?'

He wrinkled his brow in thought and it was like a Devon field freshly ploughed.

'Not to me,' he said.

'If it ever does, let me know.'

'Sure.' He hit me hard in the pit of the stomach with the edge of his hand. I gasped and then swung for the side

10

of his neck not meaning to do more than break it. He had my wrist before it was halfway there and grinned into my face. 'Time you had a work-out. You're getting slow.'

I nodded and staggered out to find a taxi.

Polyfold Plastics was in the New Cross Road just past the Underground Station. It was in a yellow brick, Victorian villa that had long forgotten better times. The garden was a twelve-foot square of cracked concrete. The lower floor was the consulting room and office of a Dr Lala Rhaja. On the hall wall was a poster urging mothers to have their children inoculated against diphtheria. Below it on a bracket was a potted geranium which needed watering. On the turn of the first floor was a door with Polyfold Plastics Limited painted on it. A card below said, Walk In.

I did. The waiting room was empty. Through a half open door on the far side of the room I could hear someone whistling mournfully. I knocked and put my head round. There were two desks in the room. One to the left of the door and the other backed up against a far window with a man sitting at it, facing me. He was in his middle thirties with crinkly, damp-looking hair, and an eagle-beaked nose topped by two very dark, very widely spaced eyes that were heavy with sadness.

He said, 'Hullo.'

I said, 'Hullo,' and decided that he might be Persian with a solid Deptford waterfront streak somewhere.

I went into the room, shut the door and then handed him one of my cards. He looked at it, pushed his lower lip up until it almost touched his nose, and then said, 'Sit down. Unless you'd rather go right away. I've got nothing helpful for you. Arnold Finch, isn't it? Nice chap. I really mean it.'

I sat down behind the other desk.

I said, 'You're Mr Cadilly?' Lancing had listed the name of the other joint director in his information.

He nodded.

I gave him a warm smile and said, 'I wonder if you would care to give me a brief pen picture of your ex-director.'

'I could write a book.'

'Just give me the chapter headings.'

'Who are you working for?'

'Solicitors. He's been left six thousand by an aunt.'

He nodded. 'I know. They've been in touch with me. Old Jessica. Arnie got her to put up a thousand towards Polyfold.'

'What plastics do you make?'

'None. We put up ideas, collect orders, farm them out. Any idea how many small plastics firms there are within a mile of here?'

'No.'

'Dozens. We're the ideas and marketing end. Arnold was brilliant. No, really. Brilliant. Could have made a pile. Then three months ago, he upped and left. Got any cigarettes?'

I threw him my packet. He took one, lit it, and left the packet lying on his desk.

'Where did you meet him?'

'Pub near the Elephant and Castle. Or what used to be the Elephant. Rare old modern muck-up they've made of that.'

I took out a notebook and pencil and stared at the blotter on the desk in front of me.

'Know anything about his private life? Friends outside of business?'

'No. He was the West End type. I'm strictly south of the river. But we got on. Pleasant chap.'

'Charmer, eh?'

'The top. When he gave it full throttle everything went down for him. Eat out of his hand. Animals, women, tough old business pappas who'd cheat their own sons. Me, you, his aunt ... any old one he met in a pub. Great gift.'

'Any special girl friend?'

12

'Not that I know. I tell you, I didn't know anything about him, except the business side.'

'What happened when he left? I mean about the business?'

'He withdrew his share. Bloody awkward, too, for me. You wouldn't have two thousand you want to invest? Good prospects.'

'I might manage fifty pounds,' I said. 'If I ever find Arnold. What reason did he give you for pulling out?'

'None.'

I looked at him, mild eyed. It was a bald word. It was categoric. But somewhere I was a little uncomfortable about it.

'None,' I said.

'That's right. Just said he was going, wanted his money, and that was that.'

'Didn't you press for reasons?'

He looked at me with damp eyes and waggled his head.

'I'm not the pressing kind, Mr Carver. Only when I know it'll work – and Arnie was way out of my class.'

'Well, I think I would have wanted to know.'

'Of course, Mr Carver – but that's your profession. You got to know to earn your money.'

'Where did he live – while he was working with you?'

'Don't know. We didn't have any social contacts other than a drink in a pub at lunch time. He travelled about a lot for us, getting orders. Good salesman. Charm the birds out of trees.'

I said, 'Why do you think he hasn't come forward to collect six thousand quid?'

'Easy. He just doesn't know about it. Abroad somewhere. If he knew – he wouldn't waste time.' He stood up. 'Sorry I can't help you more. How much a year do you make in your game?'

'Not enough.' I stood up.

'We're all struggling,' he said.

'Some more than others,' I said. 'But the race is not

necessarily to the swift.' I took a step forward and picked up my cigarettes from his desk.

'Too true.'

He opened the office door for me and I went out. He watched me across the outer office. I opened the door, turned and gave him a smile and then went out, pulling the door after me but, as it closed, still keeping the handle turned over in my hand so that I could open it again without any lock click. I stood there and I heard the door to his inner office close. At the sound I opened the outer door and slipped back into the office. It wasn't that he'd said anything that made me doubt him. It was pure habit, and habit is something you can't control.

I went quietly to the door of his office and bent down and looked through the key hole.

He was sitting at his desk, telephone receiver in his hand as he dialled a number.

After a moment or two, he said, 'Ascanti Club ?... I want to speak to Mr Billings ... Oh.' It was clear from his face that Mr Billings wasn't there. 'Then get me Miss Brown ... Yes, Miss Bertina Brown.' He sat back cuddling the receiver against his ear and began to smile. After a moment, he said, 'Hullo, love. Cadilly here. Look love, tell Mr Billings I've just had a bloke here inquiring for Arnie ... Now don't fuss. He's from the solicitors – they've got tired of advertising.' He squinted at my card on the desk. 'Name of Carver. Carver and Wilkins, in Northumberland Avenue. Nice polite chap, doing an honest job. But I thought Mr Billings should know. What?' he sat listening for a moment and the smile on his face broadened and he began to laugh. 'Sure ... Just think of it – six thousand quid and Arnie can't get his fingers on it ...' He laughed, shaking his head. 'God, that's a rich one. Six thousand – What?' His face went mock solemn. 'All right, love. Just my sense of humour. What? ... That's right. Carver ... 'Bye.' He put the telephone down and sat back and beamed. Then he began to chuckle. A real, fat, innocent, pleasure-packed chuckle.

I went. Outside, Spring had come back. The sky was a delicate smoky London blue, and from a window cornice above Lala Rhaja's surgery a barrel-chested pigeon was giving with an Indian lullaby. I walked the three hundred yards to the Underground Station for exercise, then decided to be spendthrift and caught a taxi. I now had a strong feeling that this might well be more than a fifty-pound job. Apathy, Wilkins might have been glad to hear, had given way to excitement.

TWO

Coffee with Miss Brown

I HAD AN early spaghetti bolognese and three glasses of
chianti in the King's Road, and then walked to my flat.
The flat was near the Tate Gallery; a bedroom, sitting-
room, bathroom and kitchen. I'd spent a lot of money on
it – at the odd intervals when I'd had a lot of money – and
it was always untidy. From the sitting-room window, by
craning my neck, I could just see the river. I cleaned my
teeth to get rid of the tarty roughness of the chianti and
then sat down at the telephone.

I put a call through to Scotland Yard, to a man I knew.
After all it was a basic check. And anyway, when there
is the slightest fishy smell around, it is always wise for my
kind to ring them. They've got big, strong feet but they
still don't like people treading hard on their toes.

'Arnold Finch,' I said. 'Care to give me a clearance?'

'Not tonight, old man. Up to my ears. Ring you tomorrow.'

'At the office then. How's crime?'

'Escalating.' He rang off.

I sat back and did some more thinking. Bertina Brown.
It was a nice name. The Ascanti Club I knew. But I didn't
intend to do anything about either of them that evening.

I watched television until about ten and then I put on a
duffel coat and a cloth cap, checked I had all I wanted in
the pockets of the coat and went out. I took a taxi to the
New Cross Underground Station and from there walked
down to Cadilly's office. There was a light showing through
the fanlight. I went in. I could hear a couple of women
chatting somewhere at the end of the passage. Maybe that
was where Lala Rhaja kept his harem.

16

Cadilly's office door was no problem. He probably didn't care. He wouldn't be the kind to leave any cash around at night. I went in with the light of a torch. There was a venetian blind at the window of his office and I dropped it and closed the slats.

There was no safe. Just his desk and a big filing cabinet. Nothing was locked. I went through everything, starting with the correspondence flimsies. It was a genuine business all right, and Arnold Finch had worked for it. There were letters to firms advising them that he would be calling, some of them chatty letters showing that he had known various managers for some time. The only foreign business they did was with a firm near Killarney in Ireland. Polyfold Plastics were their agents for the supply of plastic cases for transistor radios – these cases were made by a firm in Stepney. There was quite a bit of business and in the last year Arnold Finch had been over to Killarney six times.

I found the books of the company in the left-hand bottom big drawer of the desk. Two big ledgers. All very neat and tidy and – I guessed – kept by Cadilly. I could read accounts. If you're really interested in money, it's a thing that comes naturally.

Both lads had put a couple of thousand each to start the company – and it took me ten minutes to make sure that, so far as the books were concerned, there had been no capital withdrawal of Finch's share when he had left. He mightn't work there any longer, but he still had a stake in it.

The only other items of interest were in another drawer of the desk – but professionally they were no help because they concerned Cadilly's sex life. I didn't waste too much time on them. I put everything back, neat and tidy as I'd found it, ledgers, files, letters, photographs and the well thumbed erotic books.

The two women were still chatting and laughing when I left but now the passageway was thick with a strong smell of curry.

17

I went home and slept like an innocent. I was in the office at nine-thirty. Wilkins was already there.

I said to her, 'There's a girl called Bertina Brown who uses the Ascanti Club. She isn't listed in the phone book. I don't care how you get it but I want her home number. And when you get it, phone Billy Stone and get the address that goes with it.'

If you had a telephone number but no address – and if you had a fiver – then you could always get the address from Billy. He did well, and changed his Jaguar every second year.

I put my feet up on the desk and looked at the paper. The world was still in its usual turmoil, and some cement shares that a grateful client had tipped for me had gone down again, a shilling. You'd have thought that cement was like bread, something people just had to have.

After about twenty minutes Wilkins came back in holding a slip of paper. On it were Bertina Brown's telephone number and a Kensington address.

She said, 'Billy says it will cost you ten pounds. It's an unlisted number.'

She went and got my coat for me and held it up. She gave me a tight-lipped look and said, 'You're just excited – about a girl in a night club. You're having all sorts of romantic notions. You've got that look. Oh, I know it. Ninety per cent of the work that comes in here is routine, dull. Why don't you face it? No, not you. Always you're hoping for the big excitement, for the big money.'

'Why not? Anyway, I've a feeling that there may be more in this than a straightforward rent-paying job.'

I went down to get a taxi. The brass plate outside the street door – Carver and Wilkins – was dewed with sleet. I turned into the tobacconist's next door and bought a fresh supply of cigarettes to feed to nicotine-starved informers. The blonde behind the counter smiled at me over the nursery slopes and said, 'When are we going to have that weekend in Brighton?'

I said, 'As soon as business slacks off.'

18

She said, 'Don't make it too long. I don't want to be pushed around in a bath chair.'

I went out, speeded by a fat wink from her, and found a taxi which, eventually, dropped me at the top of Montpelier Square.

It was a nice house, squashed up a little, like an old maid shrugging her shoulders, and the door was green with a thin black line around it. The brass knocker was in the shape of a *putto* with little sprouts of wings and a knowing leer to the mouth. There was a row of brass name plates let into the stonework. The second from the top read – Miss Albertina Brown. I pressed the bell alongside it. The door swung open and I went in.

The hall had a green marble-topped table and over it a wall mirror with an ormolu frame. Through a half-open door beyond it came a faint smell of incense and the sound of a droopy voice, saying, 'But Charles, the whole thing these days is that it is not enough to form ... to create ... to fashion ... a static shape. Everything is in a flux and the shape must move ... must change ... must alter ...'

I went quickly up the blue-carpeted stairs.

There was a brass plate like the one on the street door and a push button under it. I pressed it and it sounded like a fire alarm going off. As the echoes died away the door opened.

That was the trouble with my life. Doors were always opening to reveal strange people standing on the threshold. A good many of them I disliked at once, some of them I learned to tolerate, but a few – say one every two years – made me immediately conscious of the back of my ears. The alarm bell tolls, and if you've got any sense you know you should start trampling your way to the emergency exit.

She had cornflower blue eyes, candy floss spun blonde hair and wore black tights and an even tighter black jumper affair that left her arms bare. The arms were a golden brown.

I didn't get a chance to make a fuller inventory because

19

in a voice which I thought had a touch of unfriendliness in it, she said, 'Yes?'

Knowing the world's need for friendship, I gave her a big smile and said, 'I'm your long lost uncle from Australia. But you can't ever take over my sheep farm. The life's too hard for a girl.'

Closing the door, she said, 'Go away and take your sheep with you.'

Just in time, I got my foot in the crack and she jammed the door hard against it.

'All right,' I said, 'Let's make a fresh start.'

I handed her one of my cards.

She glanced down at it and then her face came up quickly to me and she was frowning and there were the most delightful little thought wrinkles across her brow.

She handed the card back to me, eased the door pressure off my foot a little, and said, 'I've got nothing to say to your kind. Now, go away.'

'Okay,' I said. 'But it's a bit hard when I'm just trying to find someone to tell them they've been left six thousand pounds.'

I pulled my foot out of the door as I saw her hesitate.

'What did it say on the card?'

'Carver and Wilkins. I'm Carver. Rex. Housetrained and with very reasonable manners.'

'Carver . . .' She said it speculatively to herself and then looked me over slowly. I didn't mind how long she took, because I was doing the same to her, and trying to decide why girls wore jumpers like that. It certainly wasn't to conceal anything. As a corollary, I knew that she was probably remembering hearing my name from Cadilly.

I said, 'I won't waste any of your time. Just a few simple questions. I'm only—' I said humbly, 'trying to do an honest job of work.'

She made some decision, and probably, too, decided some line of action, for she opened the door and stepped aside for me to enter.

As I did so, she said, 'Inquiry agent, eh? Shouldn't you wear a raincoat and a slouch hat?'

I said, 'I keep them for the Soho beat.' And I knew that she had decided to play it friendly and say nothing that was going to be of any damned help to me.

She gave a little giggle and went down a narrow hallway ahead of me. She looked just as good from behind, and I wondered why I always had to be so impressionable.

The hallway had one of those Chinese horse drawings in a red frame, and a bowl of artificial irises on a very nice little antique table with brass-bound legs. Beyond it was a sitting room, big and lofty, with a divan, silk-covered in black and yellow stripes and two big armchairs to match. The curtains were the same material and there was a black carpet. The fireplace was hidden by a low Japanese screen. Two doors led off the room and both were open. Through one was coming a whiff of steam and I could hear an electric kettle screaming its head off. Through the other I could see the end of an unmade bed. Striped dressing-gown and striped pyjamas were thrown across the end, big yellow, green and red stripes.

She said, 'I was just going to make some coffee. Would you like some?'

'Thank you.'

She moved away from me, closed the bedroom door in passing and went into the kitchen. In her place I would have wanted a little time to think, too. I sat down in an armchair and felt my ears settling down a bit.

Her head came briefly round the kitchen door and she smiled and said, 'I'm sorry. It's only Nescafé.'

It was a nice smile, wrinkling up her small nose and giving a glimpse of a row of very even white teeth while at the same time she managed a tantalizing flicker of eyelashes over her blue eyes.

A few minutes later she came back, carrying a tray with two mugs on it, a silver sugar bowl, and a little china milk jug. She put the tray on a table by my side and said, 'Go ahead. I'll have mine later, when it's cooler.'

As I put milk into my coffee, she lay down on her back on the carpet and said, 'Don't pay any attention to me. I never miss my morning exercises.'

I said, 'Pity. I've done mine – otherwise I would join you.'

She said, 'So you're an inquiry agent? Why don't you inquire?'

She began to go through a set of exercises with great concentration. It was impossible not to pay attention to her. I just watched and tried to do business at the same time. But she wasn't fooling me. She had linked me with Cadilly, and she had already worked out her line of conduct. Take it nice and easy, be natural and innocent, she had no doubt said. Don't get flustered. And lying on her back was a good way of not letting me get a good look at her pretty face. There's nothing like the face for giving away thoughts.

I said, 'I'm working for a firm of solicitors who want to trace a man called Arnold Finch. His aunt has died and left him six thousand pounds.'

Lying on her back, her legs doing a bicycling movement five inches from my nose, she said without pause or special emphasis, 'Lucky man. I've got an aunt in Canada – she's always writing to borrow from me. But what has this Arnold Finch got to do with me?'

She rolled over on her tummy, stretched behind her shoulders with her arms, got hold of her toes and began to rock gently. I noticed that she was wearing an engagement ring, a gold band with what looked like a big blue Cape diamond.

'From information received,' I said, 'I was led to believe that you knew him.'

Still rocking, so that I could not see her face, which was a pity, she said, 'Somebody's pointed you in the wrong direction. I don't know any Arnold Fitch.'

'Finch,' I said.

'Finch,' she said.

It wasn't good enough. She'd got it right the first time.

22

It was faulty psychology to pretend to get it wrong the second.

'Sure?' I asked.

'Absolutely.'

She tired of rocking and began to do press-ups.

'Well, that's tough on me,' I said. 'I thought you'd be the end of the trail and I'd pick up my fifty quid fee without more bother.'

'Sorry.'

She was going up and down like a professional gymnast and, while I watched the jumper work its way free from her trouser top to show a nice crescent of golden brown flesh, I was thinking how much Miggs would have approved of her.

I said, 'My informant was quite definite.'

'So am I,' she said. 'Brown's a common name. There's never been any Finch in my life.'

I knew she was lying, of course. Not only because I'd heard Cadilly talk to her about Arnold, but because I had just stubbed out my cigarette in the ashtray on the small table at my side. It was decorated in black and red wash, and showed Bacchus sitting on a rock while a couple of nymphs draped themselves over him. At the base of the rock were the initials J. F. It had to be a present from Arnold.

I said, 'Well, it doesn't matter. I often find myself down dead ends.'

She collapsed to the carpet, rolled over and sat up on her haunches. She pushed a lock of hair from her eyes. The interrogation was over. She could show her face now.

'If I could have helped, I would,' she said.

'Oh, I'm sure.' I gave her a big smile. 'Nice ring you've got there.'

She looked down at her hand at the ring and then, as though it were something she'd long forgotten about, she said, 'Oh, that.'

I reached forward and retrieved a comb which had fallen from her hair and gave it to her.

'I hope he's worthy of you,' I said.

She gave me a warm smile. 'I've almost forgotten what he looked like. He didn't want it back, so I kept it. I wear it when I don't feel like fighting the wolves off.'

'If there's a vacancy going . . . ? All my life I've been looking for the right girl. You know . . . love is the thing. Two hearts beating as one.'

She said, 'You should write poetry. And I think you should go.'

'If you say so. But I haven't finished my coffee.'

She stood up and put milk and sugar into her mug on the tray. Then she cradled the mug against one cheek to test the temperature and eyed me very steadily. She wasn't worried about me now. I'd accepted her word about Arnold Finch and she was relaxed.

She said, 'You men are all the same. Don't you ever think of anything else?'

I said, 'There are times when it's difficult. You might go farther and fare worse. I'm not so stuck on exercises as you, but I'm in fair nick and always ready to give a demonstration run.'

She said, 'You're a pushing bastard, aren't you? I can read every thought in your head and the answer is no.'

I stood up and shrugged my shoulders. 'Not my day,' I said. 'Here I am bearing gifts, six thousand quid for some lucky guy who, apparently, couldn't care less, and a heart-ful of love and devotion just waiting for some girl I can lavish it on.'

She nodded her head. 'I know. Life's rough.'

She began to move across the room.

'Where are you going?' I asked.

'To open the door for you to go out. I was taught it was polite.'

She opened the door into the hall.

I followed her. In the hall, I said, 'What are you doing for dinner tonight?'

She said, 'Eating, I hope.'

I said, 'Coincidence. That's what I had in mind.'

24

She said, 'That's as far as the coincidence goes.'

She opened the outer door.

I said, 'I'm sorry to have bothered you.'

She smiled. 'You haven't bothered me at all.'

'Not even the tiniest bit?'

She smiled, taking it as a joke, but I thought I caught just the flicker of a shadow of speculation in her eyes.

She said, 'Goodbye, Mr Carver.'

I said, 'Au revoir, Miss Brown,' and stepped out. The door closed gently behind me. As I went down the stairs I could feel my ears slowly coming back to normal, and I was prepared to bet that she was already back in the sitting-room picking up the cream-coloured telephone. It was a pity the Post Office didn't do them in stripes or she would have had one. Anyway, what was all this about Arnold Finch? Something was wrong somewhere. But where did she fit in? She didn't strike me as the kind of girl who – I cut off the character analysis sharply. Character reading was a mug's game. The only definite thing about her was that she had made the back of my ears burn. Just be content with that for the time being, I told myself.

Back at the office to my surprise I found that Wilkins was out to lunch. I hadn't realized that it was so late, and then I remembered that I'd walked all the way back from Montpelier Square in a pleasant daze, thinking about Bertina. Not just about her, her general impact on me, but the fact that she had been lying about Arnold Finch. I could have called her bluff, of course, but generally speaking I'd found that it was better to say nothing when there was no obvious reason sticking out for the lie.

I stuck my feet up on my desk and thought. I had to move a little bowl of lilies of the valley which Wilkins had put there. Bertina Brown. Somehow the name worried me. It was still worrying me when the phone went in the outer office. Wilkins had forgotten to switch the connexion through. I went out and sat at her desk.

It was the man from Scotland Yard.

'Arnold Finch,' he said. 'Nothing on him.'

'Pity.'

'Why?'

'I don't know. But I get a feeling it is.'

'You should work here. Nothing is nothing. But if there's something – then it means work. My wife is having to explain to the kids who the strange man is that comes home twice a week.' He hung up.

I stared at the office door and asked it why Arnold Finch didn't want to pick up six thousand pounds. Three seconds later part of the answer came through the door. Without knocking a man walked in.

He gave the impression that he not only had to stoop to get through the doorway but also had to turn slightly sideways. He wore a loud check suit, and a bowler hat whose weathered shine came from the great wide spaces of turf and greyhound meetings. He had big brown eyes that not even Red Riding Hood would have trusted, and his face had a whisky flush that must have meant a lot to the Distillers' Company.

He stopped two feet in front of me, kept his hat on and his hands in his coat pocket.

'Carver? Rex Carver?' The words had the real gravelly, sand-collapsing sound.

'Yes.'

'What you doing there then?'

I said, 'I'm sitting in for my secretary while she's out having lunch for me. Next question?'

'Anyone in there?' He tipped his head towards my room.

'Just a bunch of lilies of the valley.'

That puzzled him. He went to my door, opened it and grunted.

He turned and came back to me and I stood up. I still had to look up to him, but not so far. He pulled a fist like a Bath chap from his pocket and, with a very fast movement of his thick fingers, fanned out a dozen or so five-pound notes.

26

'Money!' I smiled. 'You giving it away?'

'That's the idea.' He handed it over to me and I was too polite to count it but it couldn't have been less than fifty pounds. I put it in my pocket.

'Thank you.'

'Pleasure.' Then he gave a momentary frown and said, 'Get it straight though, I'm just doing a friend a favour. Don't know what it's all about but I got clear instructions.'

'What are friends for except for doing favours for?'

He started to work that one out and then let it go, and said, 'Arnie don't want to be found, not even if the Bank of England wants to make him Governor.'

'I see.'

'Good. That's all right, then. You just play around a bit, then say no soap to the solicitor boys and take their money.'

'Wouldn't that be dishonest?'

'What's that got to do with it?' He really was surprised. But it was a good question.

'I'm not sure,' I said. 'But I get a feeling I don't like it.'

He looked at me hard, and then shook his head and his big dewlaps wobbled.

'You got the money,' he said. 'You behave. Arnie don't want to be found.'

'Arnie's going to be found,' I said.

'You insisting on that?'

'Yes.'

'You're nuts.'

'I know. But I get that way sometimes. I've been trying to break myself of it for years.'

His other hand came out of his coat pocket and he looked down at it for a moment, like a young girl admiring an engagement ring – but it wasn't any thin gold band with a big blue Cape diamond. It was a made-to-measure – had to be with his fist – brass knuckle duster. He started to come round the desk for me and I obliged him by getting out into the open first and moving close to him.

No amount of training would have ever put him in the

Miggs class. He swung at me and the air could have been thick treacle he was so slow. I took his wrist and turned my shoulder into his chest, flexed my knees and let the weight come ... Nice and easy, I could hear Miggs saying ... No hurry. Let the other guy's weight and momentum save your own muscles ...

He went clean over the desk and hit the filing cabinet behind it with his head.

I'll say this for him, he wasn't the kind who took no for an answer the first time out. He came back at me, pushing the big desk aside like an apple box, and tried again.

I had to steer him a bit this time because I didn't want him to go through the half-glass door. There was going to be hell from Wilkins anyway over the filing cabinet. He hit the wall and smashed the glass of a framed photograph of Wilkins's father's last ship, which meant big trouble. He lay on the ground, bent up a bit against the wall, and I could hear the air going from him.

I picked up his bowler hat, opened the door, and gave him a tap on the shin with my left toe.

'Help me up,' he said.

'You can manage,' I said, and held the door wider.

He managed and I handed him his hat. He half turned in the doorway.

'You're in trouble,' he said.

'Who isn't?'

He held out his hand. 'If you're not playing – hand the money back.'

I shook my head. 'That's my usual fee for a five-minute work out.'

'But that's bloody dishonest.'

'Try suing me.' I moved for him but he went out fast.

THREE

A Minnow amongst the Tiger Barbs

FROM MY flat, around six, I put in a call to Kent on the
off chance of catching Manston at home. Manston was an
old friend of mine. He was also in the same line of business
as I was – though in a much higher bracket and his monthly
cheque came fat and regularly from the Treasury. What he
didn't know about London night life would have made
quick and dull reading.

'Ascanti Club,' I said. 'I suppose you're a member?'

'Yes. Why?'

'Would you phone them and tell them I'm your guest
this evening and that you'll be joining me later?'

'Yes. Though I shan't be.'

'I'll manage once I'm in.'

He laughed and rang off.

I got there just after half past nine and in the pockets of
my dinner jacket I carried nothing more offensive than a
razor blade in a plastic holder, a handy bunch of keys, and
a propelling pencil with a tiny torch light in the end. The
place was just off Curzon Street and the entrance hall had
a carpet so deep with pile that snow shoes would have
been a help. There was a flunkey in green livery and pow-
dered wig, with a starchy manner and a slight cockney
accent who checked a big register to verify that Manston
had spoken for me.

I did a right-hand turn down a passageway hung with
shaded red lights and big gold-framed old masters, and
found the bar. Long red velvet curtains fell from the ceiling like Napoleon's bedroom, and there was a big fish tank
along one wall, about four feet deep, full of tropical fish
and waving water plants. The bar was a great curving

run of marble with two white-coated barmen behind it. One of them gave me a big smile, full of discreet friendship, fixed me a whiskey and soda and handed me so little change from a ten-shilling note that I had to pocket it because I knew he would be offended if I pushed it back to him as a tip. Old Lancing was going to cut up rough about this evening's expenses. After a couple of sips of whiskey my eyes got accustomed to the gloom and I saw that there were about a dozen people in the place, most of them sitting in scallop-shell shaped alcoves round the room. Through a half curtained archway I got a glimpse of the dining-room with a small dance floor isolated in the middle. The band was playing softly something too old fashioned for me to remember. The head waiter was in the bar taking an order for dinner at one of the alcove tables with a gold-and-leather-bound menu that he opened reverently as though it were an illuminated missal.

An elderly, parchment-faced number, a few feet up the bar from me, with an evening tie that drooped like hound's ears, began to talk to the barman about tropical fish. It wasn't a particularly fascinating conversation but it was the only one I could overhear in the cathedral hush, so I listened. Blue gouramis were bubble nesters, but it was a good thing to remove the females after spawning. Papa gourami could look after the young on his own. And then there was something about cherry barbs, which at first I thought might be a new drink, but turned out to be fish from Ceylon. The barman preferred tiger barbs that came from Malaya, though apparently they were pretty tough numbers in a community – confirmed fin-nippers.

This vellum-faced number turned to me, realizing I was eavesdropping, and said pleasantly, 'You like fish?'

'Only fried,' I said.

'Waggish,' he said, smiled and ignored me. They started to talk about something called *tanichthys albonubes* so I strolled over to the dining-room archway. There were quite a few people dining already and I was just in time to catch the first cabaret.

There was a conjurer, a young man in top hat and tails, spurting a bright line of chatter while he kept the cards and the silk handkerchiefs flowing. He got very little attention compared with the smoked salmon, the vichyssoise and the tournedos Rossini.

But the next act really did stop the clatter of cutlery. They were two Chinese girls, in neck-high yellow silk gowns and tight trousers, called Suma and Lian. I'd seen a notice in the hallway saying that this was a return appearance by popular request. Which was Suma and which was Lian was impossible to say for they were as alike as split peas – or maybe it should have been split rice. I stood just back from the doorway of the dining-room and watched them and the vellum-faced number came up alongside me and watched them too. He seemed to know all about them, and kept up a low running commentary, which I could have done without.

One of them played a three-stringed Chinese banjo, called *san hsien*, my friend informed me, and the other a Chinese dulcimer, a *yang ch'in*, having sixteen sets of strings, four in each set, and played with two bamboo beaters. Soon after they started to play he stopped talking. To begin with they sang some catchy little tinkly, temple-bell number in Chinese, probably something about the moon over the yellow river or goodbye to Formosa. Then – as one of them explained in good English – they played a Chinese harvesting celebration and there was a lot of quiet giggling and nods between them and they both moved in a rather stiff, formal dance as they sang.

After this one of them came forward alone – Suma, my friend said – and accompanied by her sister on the banjo sang in English a little number they had written themselves. It really had something. The kind of thing that if you'd had three drinks and were feeling down would have you bawling your eyes out. She just stood there with the lights moving slowly over her dark hair and, in a husky, damp sort of voice that made me think of loneliness and back streets, sang of young lovers with nowhere to go but a

31

park bench, and littered grass under the sooty branches of plane trees – and it went straight to my heart. It touched the other people there, too – which was a comfort because sometimes I think that I am too emotional for my own good. She stirred up everything that people thought they had learned to forget; the moments of heartache and innocence that everyone knows must be kicked aside if you're going to get anywhere and have a big investment folio and a place in the world.

When she finished, she got a big hand. But nothing lasts. As Suma and Lian went off, I could see the glasses of wine being reached for, the knives cutting into the tepid *poulet de Bresse*, and the chatter broke out like a grey sea washing over dirty pebbles as the crowd got back to the real things of life.

The man at my side said, 'The last time they were here they used a four-stringed moon guitar, *y'ueh k'in*. But the really interesting thing is the reed instrument. According to tradition, the Emperor Huang-ti sent his minister . . .'

God knows where he sent him because I was on the move. In the far corner of the dining-room Bertina had just sat down by herself at a small table. I stood in front of her and gave her a warm, spaniel smile begging not to be kicked before I could speak. She was wearing a plain black gown, cut low enough, and long silver earrings that hung dead still as she looked at me.

I said, 'Happy coincidence,' and, not knowing I was going to do it, reached for her hand and kissed it.

It was a long time since I'd seen a girl look so surprised. She stared at her hand where I'd kissed it and then up at me.

'It's all right,' I said. 'It's not the kiss of death.'

She said, 'What are you doing here?' She was worried, I could see. As she spoke she looked around the place as though she was searching for someone. This moment, I'd guessed, had not been covered in the brief she had been given about me since my visit to her flat.

'I'm having dinner with a man who is a member,' I said.

'But he hasn't turned up. What about you – have you been stood up, too?'

'I work here,' she said, and it sounded more like her normal voice.

A waiter floated up to the table.

I said to her, 'Have you eaten yet?'

'Yes.' Then to the waiter she said, 'The usual, Alfredo.' The waiter gave a little nod and then to me said, 'And monsieur?'

'A dry sherry,' I said.

I sat down at the table, lit a cigarette for her and asked, 'What work?'

She gave me a long look.

'Dog's body. Girl Friday. Anything which comes along. Order the flowers and arrange them. Check the bills. Bully caterers. I make thirty quid a week, plus tips – which I have to declare for tax. And sometimes if play in the gaming room is slow I play for the house to help get things warmed up. What else do you want – my girdle size?'

Oh yes, now she had firmly decided how to handle me.

Alfredo floated up at this moment with my sherry and a Guinness in an enormous glass goblet for her.

I said, 'You believe in keeping your strength up.'

'In this place it is a must.'

I said, 'Do you think you'll be strong enough to dance when you've finished it?'

She said, 'You're a great one for cutting corners. What makes you think I want to dance with you?'

'It's an experience no girl should miss. What's the matter? You got to get permission first?'

'Of course not. What are you getting at?'

'Well, to be very frank, I get the feeling that you're having to put in a lot of hard work to be natural with me.'

'I certainly didn't expect to see you here.'

I stood up. 'This, I think, is a slow fox-trot. Always brings out the best in me. You should try it. It's no good trying to kick against coincidence. Just go with it.'

I didn't expect her to, but she came into my arms and we

33

were away. We went round in silence for a while, and I just let myself go. The backs of my ears were glowing nicely and she felt good in my arms as anything I could remember for years and years. And I was glad of the silence because I was wondering what a nice girl like her could possibly be mixed up in. One thing I did know was that for the moment she had decided to let things move naturally. I wasn't asking any awkward questions and my manners were reasonably good. I was a fair dancer, too.

The third time round she must have been feeling more relaxed in herself and I suppose she thought she ought to do something to keep somewhere near the terms of the brief she had been given.

She said, 'Who's your friend? The one you're waiting for.'

'A man called Manston. He's been a member for years.'

She said, 'If he doesn't turn up, you know you won't be able to stay here. You've got to be a member.'

'Well, if he doesn't, I'll sit outside and wait to take you home in a taxi.'

She drew away a little and smiled at me. 'A taxi is the last place I'd trust myself with you. Are you always like this – pushing? Busting into no entry streets?'

'Only sometimes. Usually in the Spring. Is it okay about the taxi?'

She stopped dancing. We were alongside our table.

'I shouldn't think so. And now, if you'll excuse me, I've got work to do.'

Before I could say anything, she was gone across the floor, leaving half a glass of Guinness still in her goblet.

I finished my sherry. There was an hour before the second cabaret came on, so I went down to the gaming room. There wasn't any doubt in my mind that somewhere on the premises a little conference was taking place about Carver.

I bought myself five pounds' worth of chips and lost the lot in ten minutes at roulette. I didn't care for the place much. I'd been in Methodist chapels that were more exciting. The kind of gambling I liked was a Miggs poker school where you were free to laugh or curse aloud at your cards. So, I went back to the bar, sat in the alcove by the fish tanks and ordered a brandy.

While I was drinking it, I saw one of the flunkeys from the hall come to the main door of the bar and begin to look around the room. He made a half circle from his left with his eyes, over the bar and then found me. He didn't bother to complete the full circle, but turned and went out. The conference, I decided, had broken up, and instructions had been issued.

Five seconds later, a big, well-preserved man of about sixty came into the room. He crossed slowly and sat down at the next table to me. He was white-haired, well groomed, wore a dark blue dinner jacket which showed an inch of immaculate cuffs caught with onyx links. His face was big, heavy and imperious. Given a crown of bay leaves he could have doubled for Nero. He settled his bulk in the gilded chair with a small sigh, pulled out a crocodile cigar case and began to go through the ritual with a cigar cutter, gold naturally.

The barman materialized alongside him and said, 'Good evening, Mr Billings.'

In a slow, senatorial voice, echoing with authority nicely framed with friendliness, he said, 'Evening, Jorgens. Champagne and vodka.'

Remembering Cadilly's telephone call, I was pretty sure now that the chairman of the conference had come to look me over.

He got his cigar going without hurry. Jorgens brought him his drink. He sipped at it, gave another little sigh of pleasure, as though somehow it was the one thing he'd been waiting for to put the crown of contentment on a well-filled day. But he didn't fool me. He was eighteen inches from me, and I knew he was wondering how to begin a conversation.

I sipped my brandy in time with his second go at the Russian nitroglycerine he was drinking, and then I pulled out my cigarettes, stuck one in my mouth and went through a pantomime of discovering that I hadn't got any matches.

A gold lighter came slowly through the air and flame spurted in front of my nose.

I lit my cigarette and said, 'Thank you very much.'

'Not at all.' He slewed a little in his chair to get a better look at me, and gave me the edge of a smile. Then he said, 'You must be a new member? I haven't seen you here before.'

'Guest,' I said, and added, 'You must have been a member for some time if you can spot the new boys so quickly.'

'Quite a time,' he said.

I had the feeling that while he wanted to give me the once over, he still didn't want to get in too deep. For my part I decided that maybe this was the moment not to hold my cards too close to my chest. A frontal attack can sometimes pay dividends.

'Actually,' I said, 'I'm partly here on business. Maybe you could help me? I'm looking for a man called Arnold Finch who, I'm told, might have been a member here once.'

I handed him one of my cards and he took it carefully by one corner and studied it.

'Interesting profession,' he said.

'Frustrating is a better word. Arnold Finch has been left six thousand pounds by an aunt. I want to tell him the good news. But I can't find him – and he doesn't answer any press advertisements. Do you recall anyone of that name?'

'I'm sorry I never heard of him.'

'That's the answer I get everywhere.'

'Sad for him. It's a lot of money. I'm sure if he knew he would materialize.'

'Unless someone won't let the cork out of the bottle.'

He nodded his big Nero head, turning back a little in his chair. Then he raised one hand slightly above his head. Immediately the head waiter came swimming up out of the gloom – where for sure he had been waiting for the

36

signal – and I realized that Mr Billings had satisfied his interest in me and I had been dismissed.

Over the leather-bound menu, the two began a technical conference on what Billings should eat. He ordered *quiche Lorraine,* and a half bottle of Zeltinger Schlossberg to go with it; *mignon de sole Gondolière,* and then *selle de mouton* with a bottle of Château Lafite which he wanted decanted now, and he would be in the gaming room for an hour before he dined. He got up, gave me the briefest nod, and went out of the bar. I could have kicked his broad, Roman backside. Instead I signalled to Jorgens, ordered another brandy, and when he brought it, I said, 'Who is this Billings number?'

He said, 'Sir?'

I said, 'This Billings. Who is he?'

From the look on his face you'd have thought I'd drawn the curtains of the tabernacle or something.

'Mr Ryder Billings is a member, sir.' And he melted away, but not before carefully removing the half-crown I'd left on his tray as a tip and carefully putting it by my drink. That made two brush-offs in almost as many minutes.

The third came about five minutes later. One of the green-liveried flunkeys came into the bar, peered through the smoke haze to get his bearings and then headed for me.

Standing by my table he said, with the most solicitous respect in his slightly cockney voice, 'I'm afraid, sir, that guests are not allowed to stay in the club when the member responsible for them is not here.'

'I'll bet that's just been written into the rules.'

'Sir?'

'Never mind,' I said. 'Is it okay if I finish my brandy?'

'I imagine so, sir.'

'And powder my nose on the way out?'

He was doubtful about that one, but he gave me a faint nod eventually, and then said, 'I'm very sorry about this, sir.'

'Never mind,' I said. 'I'll go quietly.'

37

He went, and then I lingered a little over the brandy because I wanted to think, and when the thinking and the brandy were done, I got up and went out into the reception hall and down a flight of marble steps to the loo.

There was a green-liveried, wigged troglodyte in charge. I washed my hands, had a new gas refill for my Ronson lighter, chatted to the troglodyte about the day's racing, decided that he probably hadn't been tipped off about the ban on me, and said, 'Need a breath of fresh air. Can I get out to the courtyard this way?'

Closing a discreet hand over my half-crown, he said, 'Through here, sir.' He opened a door on the far side of the marble hall. 'The door at the end of the passage.'

I went slowly down the passage, heard him close the door behind me and then I stopped. There was a big service lift on the left for goods that came in through the courtyard.

I got in. There were four buttons. I pressed the top one. I went up, wondering about Ryder Billings. If he didn't own the place, he certainly carried weight.

Bertina had told me she had a small office in the upper part of the building. She might still be up there, and I wanted to talk to her.

At the top there was a long corridor, very shabby, with a couple of theatrical hampers in it and a row of doors on the left. The first one had a card in a brass slot which read – Harry Levanche. That was the conjurer. I could hear someone inside whistling to himself. I guessed this was Harry, his second act over.

The next door had nothing on it and was slightly ajar. I eased it open and went in. It was clear at once that it belonged to the two Chinese girls. And equally clear that they were a very neat pair. Most theatre dressing-rooms I had been in were untidy, but here everything was in place. In fact the only thing that struck an untidy note was a large white leather handbag, looped over the back of a chair. One of the tidy girls had slipped up there. It was hanging open. Inside I could see the edge of what looked like a passport. When it comes to idle hands the Devil has long known he can rely on me. I took it out. It was a Mexican passport in the name of Suma Tung, and there was a very nice photograph of her, head and shoulders, wearing a prim little dress with a white collar. She was twenty-eight and there was an address in Mexico City and visa and douane stamps for all over the place. She was described as a singer. Tucked inside the passport were two things. The first was an air ticket, London to Shannon, for three days ahead, which was a Monday. Then there was a telegram from someone called Granero, Panama City, which read:

SS DAHLMAN DOCKS ANTWERP MAY 20.

I put the passport back, snapped a carnation from a bunch in a vase on the dressing table and put it in my button-hole, and went out.

Four yards farther up the corridor was a door marked – Office. I opened it and went in.

Bertina was sitting in a chair behind a very untidy desk and had her feet up on it. Just for a moment, before she dropped them to ground level and out of my sight, I had a nice glimpse of them.

She ran her hands back over her hair, her mouth tightened and she gave me a dark scowl and she looked for a moment like a furious schoolgirl. The back of my ears began to warm up. I liked this girl – and somewhere deep down in me was some alter ego that was prepared to lay big money that, even if there was going to prove to be something fishy in all this, she couldn't really have any true part in it. Not if it was big. She was no angel, but she just wasn't the kind that ever got really out of their depths in dark waters.

She said, 'You've got a bloody nerve.'

I said, 'What were you thinking about when I came in? From your face it seemed serious.'

She said, 'Why don't you go away and leave me alone? If you were just trying to be friendly I don't say I wouldn't be just possibly interested. But you're bothering me.'

I said, 'And you're bothering me.'

'How?'

'By not telling the truth.'

'Now I'm a liar.'

'A very attractive one.'

'About what?'

'Arnold Finch. You say you never heard of him.'

'And I damned well haven't!' She was so emphatic that it was overdone. Maybe her secret briefing said that this was a point that really must be stressed.

'His aunt – old Jessie – was a dab hand at making ashtrays. Always had nymphs and fauns and gods and goddesses over them and she always signed them J.F. She used to unload them on to friends. Personally I don't think you can have too many ashtrays around the place. You've got one. Bacchus whooping it up with a couple of girl friends. And Arnold gave it to you.'

She said, 'You've got this Linch on the brain. I bought the ashtray at . . . a . . . a . . .'

'Jumble sale?'

'Yes.'

'The name is Finch. F I N C H. Now tell the truth.'

If we'd been left alone I don't think she would have done. Clearly there was too much pressure on her. But I cherished a little hope that maybe she would like to have told me.

However, at this moment the door behind me opened and two men came in. I turned and took one look, and then I turned half back to her.

'You must have have rung a bell,' I said.

'This one,' she said and pointed to a bell push on the desk.

There was no more conversation. I was facing the bookmaker-bruiser who had paid a visit to my office. He was wearing a dinner jacket that bulged all over, and sliding out from behind him was a weasel-faced type who must have thought that I was a rabbit. He went for me with a speed that might have taken Miggs by surprise. I was suddenly sitting on the floor, wondering if I would ever breathe again, when they picked me up and carried me out and down the corridor to the lift. Bertina gave me no farewell.

The big boy started us on our way down in the lift and said happily, 'Come into the garden, Maud.' He gave me a friendly kick in the calf that dropped me to the floor again.

I was beginning to get the hang of how to breathe again when the lift stopped and they slung me out. I ricocheted off the far wall and had just enough bounce to come back and slap the edge of my hand up under big boy's chin so that he swallowed his saliva. It was a pretty feeble effort, but I was spared from more because a voice said, 'That's enough.'

I looked up from the floor where weasel-face had dropped me with a left hook that had years of training behind it. A tall, aristocratic-looking man was frowning down at me as though I was going to give the place a bad name. He said, 'Are you Mr Carver?'

I nodded.

'I'm the manager. Please come with me.' He reached down a hand and helped me up. I heard big boy begin to make some protest but the man just looked at him over my shoulder and big boy shut up.

I followed the man into the cloakroom, and he paused and said, 'Tidy up.'

I tidied myself up and got my breath back while he lit a cigarette and watched me. The green-liveried flunkey stood by the door, stiff as a ramrod, and about as high, and I didn't have to be told that he had had a raspberry.

I turned for the door, but the dark-haired man stopped me and smiling said, 'I hope you have no complaints about your treatment here?'

'None at all,' I said.

'Good.'

We went up the stairs to the reception hall. In the archway entrance to the bar was Mr Billings with the two Chinese girls, both watching me with a kind of solemn childish interest, and if you'd asked me which was Suma,

I couldn't have told. Ryder Billings looked heavily bored as though I were some net-and-trident man who'd put up a pretty poor show.

I gave the Chinese girls a beaming smile and went out and found a taxi. As usual, I got the chatty type. When I paid him off at my flat, he said, 'Somebody slugged you?'

I touched the side of my sore chin, nodded, and said, 'He was too fast for me. I'll try and do better next time.'

The cabby nodded sympathetically. 'That's the spirit, chum. Come back fighting. Over a girl was it then?'

I said, 'If you're as good with the future as you are with the past I could use you. Keep the change.'

'Thanks. Keep at it – you'll win her in the end, I'll bet.'

'No bet,' I said and went into my flat.

FOUR

Up a Gum Tree

I WAS up before Mrs Meld arrived in the morning and went along to Montpelier Square. I had rung Bertina late the previous night and the phone had not been answered. The front door of the house was open.

I went in and, as I expected, she wasn't there. The bed was made and there wasn't a thing left in her wardrobe. I went over everything carefully, and then in the bathroom in the medicine cupboard, propped against an empty aspirin bottle, I found her note. She must have had someone with her helping with the packing and keeping an eye on her, otherwise she would never have put it where I might not find it. Not that it helped much.

It read: —

> Sorry about last night.
> For your own good – keep your nose out of things. B.

Comforting. In a way. I tore it up and flushed it down the loo.

I went down the stairs. The door of the incense-burning-three-verbs-instead-of-one flat was open. Standing in front of the ormolu mirror in the hall was a willowy number with rather thin blond hair that showed a baby-pink scalp underneath. He wore a black dressing-gown and moorish slippers and was arranging a big bowl of mimosa and irises on the hall table.

He gave me a warm smile. I nodded. He said, 'Like it?'

'Exquisite,' I said, 'You've got the touch.'

'Oh, you . . .' Little crinkles of delight fanned from the corners of his eyes.

I said, 'Seen Bertina this morning?'

'No, but then one never does.'

I handed him the photograph I had of Arnold Finch.

He looked at it, but only briefly and then, as he gave it back to me, a scolding, petulant look shadowed his face.

'Don't tell me you're one of those horrid types from Fleet Street come to pester her again about that monster Arthur Fairlawn? Really, can't you leave the poor child alone?'

Suddenly I had trouble not to look at him wide-eyed with wonder, or to believe that he couldn't hear the bell that had began to ring inside my head.

'It's Arthur, not her, we're interested in,' I said.

'Then find him,' he said, and giggled. And I knew why. I gave him a wink and made for the door. Behind me I heard him call to his flat mate, 'Charles! Come here and tell me about this . . . I think I've overdone the yellow. Charles! Do come . . .'

I floated out and charged for the nearest taxi.

I had to wait fifteen minutes for Wilkins. She came in with her cold well under control, but in a filthy temper over the broken glass of her father's picture.

I said irritably, 'Go out and get a new frame and glass. Gold frame and armour-plated glass. But just now I want the newspaper files for the first week in February last.' I paused because she was giving me a long, hard look, and then I went on. 'And thank you for the lilies of the valley.'

A few minutes later I had the files on my desk and was settling down to them.

On a foggy February night two-and-a-half million pounds' worth of diamonds, industrial, had been stolen from four different diamond merchants' premises in Hatton Garden. The four offices all adjoined one another. The way the raid had been carried out was very straightforward, but a lot of planning, timing, and rehearsal must have gone before. First of all, someone had known that on the night of the raid big stocks, much bigger than usual, were being held in the offices. And somebody was either in, or knew enough about the Electricity Board, to fix a power break-down for the two hours needed for entering and opening the safes so that there was no trouble with the alarms. And somebody else had known all about the London sewer system. The gang had gone down a mile away from Hatton Garden, in the Gray's Inn Road area, and had made their way underground to a point immediately under the first of the four offices. They'd broken up through the sewer, straight through the floor of a general office, a distance of about six feet, and so into the other three offices; four working parties, each allotted an office. From the moment of surfacing like moles in the first general office, they had done the job in three hours. They'd used the latest equipment to cut open the safes. And they'd been well trained. There wasn't a fingerprint left behind, not a cigarettte stub end, nor, half a mile away, a car or lorry seen. Two-and-a-half million pounds' worth of easily marketed stuff had just disappeared.

Once the job had been done a velvet hush had fallen over everyone. Soho, North and south of the river, there was just a blank look on everyone's face. The man in charge had power and used it. Not a single one of the troops had gone on the rampage after the victory. Usually there is always some lush who gets too much beer in him and can't resist a drowsy pillow confidence to some tart on the police list. I could imagine the frustration of the police over the whole thing. They had a good idea how it had been worked and of some of the people in it, but they had nothing which would stick. It was happening more and more – the new technology in crime, and the superb planning. Layer above layer of authority, nobody knowing anyone except in the unit he worked with, and, somewhere at the top, the director-general of the whole operation. . . .

However, the police did have one thing. Arthur Fairlawn. They never made public what clue they had to him, but they made public the fact that they wanted him for questioning about the robbery – and the press had made the most of it. He was a mystery man. Known to every big crook in London, but never photographed, never fingerprinted . . . And he had a girl friend – Albertina Brown.

At least she was his last known girl friend – though she swore that she hadn't seen him for over a month, and that their friendship had come to an end sometime before that.

I sat there and read through some of the interviews the press had had with Bertina. She'd been in the public eye for over a week at the time. And somewhere in Scotland Yard she must have been questioned very, very thoroughly. By God, she'd handled me well when I had walked in and asked about Arnold Finch, because Arnie Finch just had to be Arthur Fairlawn. Now, I knew it. I knew about Arthur's double life, and I knew why it was a big laugh that he couldn't collect his inheritance. He was out of the country and never coming back.

The robbery had taken place on February 2nd, and the police had been shouting for him by February 5th. That meant he had done a skip on the 3rd or 4th. And he could have taken the diamonds with him, and what nicer cover than innocent, plastic-travelling Arnold Finch who often went to Ireland and never had any customs trouble.

I rang for Wilkins.

I said, 'You've got contacts with the Aer Lingus people?'

'Yes.'

'Check and see if a Mr Arnold Finch flew to Ireland any time between the 2nd and 5th of February last. If he did, see if you can find out if he had a hired car waiting over there. Anything they'll come across with. And if Finch did fly on any of those dates get me a flight for Monday, but make it for not later than mid-day.'

She nodded and went.

An hour later she was back. Arnold Finch had flown out on a morning flight on the 3rd February to Shannon – and he always had a hired car waiting. She handed me a slip of paper with the name of the Shannon car hire firm. They had offices in the airport building.

Then I said, 'It's the Hatton Garden thing. Arnold Finch is Arthur Fairlawn.'

'Then you should inform the police immediately.'

'And get pushed out? The papers say it was a two-and-a-half million steal. They exaggerate. Say a million. The reward for recovery on that should be at least five per cent. And recovery is my speciality.'

'You should go to the police.'

'Nonsense. There are two stockholders in this company. You and me. The first duty of a good business man is to declare a fat dividend. We need one.'

She went out, banging the door.

I picked up the phone and dialled a man I knew in Lloyds. Now that I had a lead with the smell of cash in it, I was neglecting nothing. Arthur Fairlawn had been well-known in the Ascanti Club. Bertina – said the newspaper reports – had first met him there. Anything with an Ascanti Club connexion had my interest, even Suma Tung into whose handbag I had taken a nosy peep. My Lloyds friend gave me what I wanted in a few minutes. The SS *Dahlman* was a general freighter, mixed cargo, anything she could get within limits. She was owned by Dahlman Long and Company, a London firm. Most of the time she ran a rough schedule between Hong Kong and Antwerp through the Panama Canal, picking up what charters she could on the route. Her principal charter owner on the Atlantic side was the Agencia Ganero, Panama City. He'd never heard anything fishy about her, but if I had, he'd like to know. Then he asked me if I'd like a game of golf and I said no I was going to Ireland, and he said take your sticks and try Ballybunion, the greatest golf course in the world, I said I had other fish to fry and he said be sure to remove its skirt first, and then I rang off because that kind of conversation could go on for ever . . . when you're speaking to a member of Lloyds, that is.

That done, I took my hat and went out to Wilkins.

I said, 'If anyone calls, say you haven't seen me since yesterday afternoon. Then you can ring your father and tell him only to buy smoked haddock for one. I'm taking you out to dinner tonight.'

I went down and bought some cigarettes at the shop next door, and then walked down to Miggs's place.

He was in his office doing his accounts, his face all screwed up like that chap who had to roll a stone uphill for all eternity.

I said, 'I'll buy you an abacus for Christmas.'

He said, 'You'll buy me a Guinness round the corner right now. What's a discount of one and a half per cent on three pounds eleven shillings and tuppence?'

I told him and we went round to the pub.

After we'd taken the head off our drinks, I said, 'What did you ever hear about the big diamond steal in Hatton Garden early this year?'

'Nothing. And I don't want to. It's poison.'

'Think.'

He punished the drink a bit, sucked one of his back teeth, and then said, 'It's murder even to be curious about it. So you can imagine what it must have been like to be in it and careless. Industrials are big business. They don't give the trouble that fancy stones do. No cutting, no fences. You flog 'em straight, usually to some foreign buying agency that isn't interested in asking questions.'

I said, 'Do you know anything about Arthur Fairlawn?'

'Look,' said Miggs, 'take my tip. Lay off. I told you this thing is poison.'

That night at dinner with Wilkins I got the same warning. She knew me better than Miggs so, in her way, she could punch harder.

'You're still set on going to Ireland?'

'Still set. You know the facts. Why shouldn't I? I know something the police don't. Fairlawn is Finch. Like a good business man I'm going to keep my advantage for a bit. The more I learn – the more it may be worth.'

'You could be killed. For once in your life be sensible and go to the police.'

'And get a nice big "thank you" and no more? That's no way to satisfy bank managers.'

'You're determined?'

'Yes.'

Slowly she finished her peach melba and then she said,

48

'I've booked a room for you – from tonight – at the Albion, Brighton. You can get the late train down. Stay there until it's time to come up for your plane.'

I looked at her in surprise, rusty hair, red nose, cold-misty eyes, and then I gave her hand a pat.

'Good old Wilkins,' I said. 'Come on let's dance.'

She got up and danced. It was a waltz, and she was a good dancer. Three times a year I took her out. Always to Quaglino's, which was her idea of heaven – and I suppose there are worse ideas. Always one sweet sherry before dinner. Always smoked salmon, sole, one glass of Chablis, peach melba, then a dance, then coffee, and after that a taxi to Charing Cross so that she could be back in Greenwich by eleven in time to get the old man's bedtime cocoa. I wouldn't have had her any different for a lakh of rupees. There are women and women, but damned few Wilkinses.

Before she went through the station barrier, she handed me a cloakroom ticket.

'I went round and packed your case this afternoon. It's waiting at Victoria for you. No need to go back to your flat. And be careful.'

I spent the weekend in Brighton alone. On the Monday I was in Shannon by mid-day. The rain was coming down steadily, topping up the peat bogs and making the road-side ditches run high with Guinness-coloured water.

I didn't have any trouble with the car-hire people – at least, not suspicious trouble . . . none of the, And be Jasus now, why would you be wanting to know? They remembered Mr Finch, and why not, the nice gentleman that he was, and always hired his cars from them for the Killarney trip. But when I pinned them to the February 3rd trip, there was a lot of argument because he'd driven off by himself and had never returned the car. They had had to send a man to pick it up after getting a phone call from him. And now, was it from Kenmare or Glengarriff? There were two schools of thought, but it was finally sorted out that Kenmare had been the doctor who had broken his leg walking on Macgillycuddy's Reeks . . . the great gentleman he

49

was and telling stories all the way back ... you remember now, Mike, the fine one about the padre and the Protestant minister ... I was given two or three samples of the doctor's repertoire, and finally found that Finch had left the car at a hotel in Glengarriff called O'Toole's, from where it had been collected ... And no trouble at all, sir.

So, I collected my own car, and then I waited outside the airport. I had little reason to think that there might be any connexion between Suma Tung and Arthur Fairlawn – except the Ascanti-Club-cum-Billings one – but I never minded wasting a little time on a long shot. My money was on Fairlawn, but I didn't mind having a flyer on Suma.

Suma arrived an hour after me, and was met by a chauffeur-driven car. She was wearing a little green suit with a yellow silk scarf at her throat. Her car, driven fast, went by me in a cloud of spray. I could never have kept up with it, even if I'd known where she was going. In the next four-and-a-half hours I did one hundred and fifty miles, mostly through low clouds studded with donkey carts on the wrong side of the road.

When I reached Glengarriff, to my modified surprise, Suma's car was parked outside O'Toole's Hotel, which didn't look much. In case she should be staying there, I found myself a bed and breakfast place down the road, a plate of cold mutton and boiled potatoes for dinner, and went early to bed on a lumpy mattress, listening to the rain running over the gutters.

When I woke the sun was shining cautiously, not making any big promises, and the whole house was full of a delicious smell of eggs and bacon.

Over breakfast my landlady, Mrs Leary, said, 'You'll not be staying long, I suppose?'

'It depends,' I said.

'Of course,' she said. 'But you're not for the fishing or the golf, that's plain.'

'True,' I said.

'You'd like more bacon?' She took my plate from me and went into the kitchen. I didn't protest. It was good bacon and she cooked it the way my sister in Honiton did, just on the curl and with a touch of brown to the fat. While I waited, I read a holiday information folder on Glengarriff which I'd picked up at Shannon. For some reason I don't understand I read guide books and information pamphlets the way other people go for pornography.

Glengarriff – Gleann Garbh – meaning Rugged Glen. Pop. 400. On the edge of the sea, in the lap of the Caha Mountains, a country of rare grandeur. Then there was something about rocks and boulders thrown together in tumultuous confusion – I'd like to have watched that from a safe distance – all clothed in luxuriant foliage. The harbour dotted with a hundred islets and guarded at its entrance by the loveliest of them all, Garnish Island. I liked that – in fact I could see something of the great spread of water from the window, but not much because it had begun to rain again even though the sun was shining somewhere behind us above the Caha Mountains.

The landlady came back with the bacon and said, 'Is it true what I hear about the Duke of Edinburgh, then?'

I said, 'I shouldn't think so.'

'I should hope not,' she said. 'Them dirty newspapers. And he's a fine man.'

'None finer,' I said, and added, 'They tell me that this place boasts an unusually mild climate. Sub-tropical plants flourish in the open. And all because the warm waters of the Gulf Stream lap along the shore.'

'Every word is God's truth. Though there's a touch of east in the wind this morning. That's not to say it would spoil the fishing. Are you fond of fish?'

'I am.'

'Then I'll get some for supper. There's salmon or sea trout. Or maybe mackerel, conger, pollack, whiting or mullet? Myself, there's nothing to touch hake – just plain boiled.'

'Sea trout sounds good.'

'It is that, though I doubt we'll get any, it being Tuesday.' Before I could ask why, she dumped the tomato

51

sauce bottle at my elbow. 'You should try that. The school-teacher makes it in her spare time. Tell me, is it true what them dirty newspapers are saying about your Prime Minister?'

'Probably,' I said.

'Aye,' she nodded. 'They did the same for De Valera.' She took my plate from me. 'Well, I can't stand here gossiping all day.'

Five minutes later, as I was going out of the house she called to me from somewhere at the back, 'That's your fancy is it, then? A nice piece of boiled hake?'

'Nothing finer.'

I walked up to O'Toole's. The Tung car was gone. I went into the hotel hall. Two picture-postcard stands flanked the desk. Behind was a shelf of little green plaster goblins. Below them, her back to me, was a girl setting out a tray of tweed ties and scarves.

I said, 'Is Miss Tung down yet?'

The girl turned. She was young, dark, flashing-eyed, and with a pink-and-cream complexion that only soft rain and the Gulf Stream can produce.

'Miss Tung?'

'The Chinese lady.'

'Oh yes.'

'Is she down yet?'

'She is not.'

'Having breakfast?'

'She is not.'

'I've got an important message for her.'

'Maybe, but she never stays here. Just garages the car. At least, that old devil Frost does.'

'How will I reach her?'

'Get Harry to take you out – like he did her last night.'

'Harry?'

'You might find him down at the pier where the Cork steamer used to be coming in.'

'He's a boatman?'

'You could call him that.'

52

'What do you call him?'

'He's my mother's brother and a disgrace to a decent family one way and another when the whiskey's in him. Though I'll admit when he has the money he can be generous. 'Tis no secret. What he makes of a Chinese lady, I don't know. He's always on about the Communists and the anti-blood-sports people.'

'They probably upset the fishing. Thank you very much for your help.'

'You're welcome. You're from London?'

'Yes.'

'My mother was there in service when she was young. It sounds a dreadful place.'

'It is.'

She held up a blue tweed tie. 'That would go fine with the suit you're wearing.'

I said, 'I have other suits. I might take half a dozen.'

She liked that – under the Dresden-china complexion lurked a shrewd business woman, and it was easy, while I dickered over ties, to learn that a Mr A. Finch – a great friend of mine – had stayed there for one night on the 3rd February. Just one night. Interesting.

I walked down the road towards the pier where the Cork boats used to call.

I stood above a stone slipway with three or four motor boats moored close to it and looked out over the harbour. It was more a long sea loch, studded with small islands.

As I stood there with the soft rain coming down and the shy sunlight gilding it, a man in gumboots with turned-over tops, a damp velvet jacket, wearing a Homburg hat green with age and five or six trout flies stuck in the crown, came up from the slipway, wiped the rain from his face and said with a toothy grin, 'A fine morning, sir.'

'It is that.'

'Aye, it is, and it could be better later.' He then studied me closely, little curiosity furrows creasing his brown brow, and finally went on, 'No offence, sir, but you're wearing a tie already.'

His eyes went down to the ties which I was holding absently in my hands.

'So I am,' I said, 'but I like to have spares in case the weather changes.'

'Oh, aye,' he said.

I pocketed the ties and said, 'Where's Harry this morning? I was told I could find him here.'

'I'm Harry,' he said. 'From O'Toole are you?'

'Yes.'

'I see she over-sold you on ties. She'll go far that one. Always talking of opening a shop. And she will one day. Must have over a hundred pounds in the bank already. Thinking of taking a trip, were you?'

'I was. Just around the islands. Is that all right?'

'My pleasure, sir.'

It wasn't difficult after that. Harry was a great talker. I heard all about the Chinese lady who, considering her race, was very pleasant. He'd taken her out to Gowduff Island, private property, some London millionaire's place, never there much, and nobody liked him. Often had people to stay, though in the summer more than now, and a bloody great wall round the island, which was hardly decent. Two cases she'd had, one with three red stripes on it. First he'd taken out except the staff for months. They did say that some strange things went on out there. Though he couldn't see that she looked the type, but then you couldn't tell with the Chinese.

I showed him the photograph of Arnold Finch, and asked him if he remembered ever taking him out? He gave me a shrewd look, and then said, 'It's well I remember him. Early February, and a big pig-skin case.'

Harry was a great one in suitcases.

'Ever bring him back?'

'No. But there are other boatmen. And they have their own launch. Friend of yours, sir?'

'In a way. Is there a telephone out to the island?'

'No, sir.'

He took me round Gowduff Island. The wall was about

ten feet above high water mark and tall enough to stop any climber. There was a main double iron gateway above a boat slip and through it I could see a glimpse of garden and trees, but no sign of the house. Alongside the slipway was a boathouse with an open front with an iron grill that came down into the water. Behind it I could see a motor launch, and beyond that in the back of the boathouse a half open door through which there was another glimpse of the garden.

'Don't like people trespassing,' I said.

'They do not,' said Harry. 'But that's not to say it couldn't be done if you were after one of the pheasants or wanted to do a little quiet courting with one of the housemaids that used to be there when I had a mind for that kind of sport. Will I take you to Garnish Island now? There's the finest garden there in the whole of Southern Ireland.'

So we went to Garnish Island, where Harry waited for me for half an hour while I walked round the gardens wondering what to do.

I could have landed, rung the gate bell, and asked to see Arnold Finch – but I didn't fancy that was any way to pick up a reward for stolen diamonds. At the moment I could see no advantage in frankness.

Half way back to Glengarriff, Harry said, "Tis no business of mine, but I did it once before, years ago. He paid me five pounds and he was from London, too. You can tell me to hold me tongue if I'm wrong, but he was like you, well spoken sort of, and pretending all the time that it was Garnish Island and the rare plants on his mind but not able to keep back the odd question about Gowduff. I put him ashore there at eleven and picked him up at cockbreak the next morning. And it was no surprise. You get a feeling about people. Maybe it's second sight. My mother had it and a hell of a lot of trouble it brought her at times, knowing what was going to happen, and devil a thing to be done about it, particularly with a drunken old pig like me father was. But mind you, I said afterwards, I'd never do it again for five pounds. Why a man could be letting himself in for a lot of trouble that wouldn't be worth it at that price.'

'Ten pounds,' I said.

'Ah, that's different. And, anyway, you seem a decent sort.'

'Thanks.'

'And if you don't want Mrs Leary to know, just drop out of the bedroom window on to the garden shed roof.'

Harry took me out at half-past ten. There was the odd gleam now and then of moonlight behind the bulky rain clouds and somewhere, just off the harbour mouth, the Gulf Stream was slogging away, loaded to the gunwales, no doubt, with all the elvers it was bringing back from the Sargassos, and Harry said it would be a dirty night later because the wind was beginning to set south-west into Bantry Bay, and, by God, a man must be mad to do this kind of thing for ten pounds when for all he knew I might be a crook or something. A strong smell of whiskey wafted down on the night air from him, and I remembered the character reference his niece at O'Toole's had given him, when the drink was in him. In fact, not to put too fine a point on it, I wasn't too sure of Harry at all. He was just too convenient, but for the moment I was prepared to go along with him, fatalistically, which is the way I go most of the time since it saves me the trouble of planning too much.

The idea, he said, was this: you stripped to your underpants, or to the hide if you had the mind, rolled your clothes in a bundle at the gate at the head of the slipway and tossed the lot over. Then you took to the water, swam to the iron grill of the boathouse and then duck-dived down for a couple of feet and went under the grill. The door at the back of the boathouse was never locked. At cock-break you repeated the process in reverse.

He shut off the motor as we came into the island, handed me a whiskey bottle and recommended a long swig, since it was early in the year yet for bathing. I took his advice and shuddered as the whiskey hit me. It was like liquid dynamite and, he said, was made by a friend of his in the Bord Fáilte Eireann.

He dropped me at the foot of the slipway, then pushed off with the boathook and disappeared into the night. I went up to the double gates and tried them. They were locked. From inside the grounds I could see a far light that looked as though it were coming from a window. I stripped to the hide because I didn't fancy going around with wet pants in my jacket pocket, made a bundle, and tossed it over the wall at the side of the gate. Harry was dead right about it being early in the year for swimming. I shivered as I slipped into the water and tried to warm myself up with the thought of the diamond reward. Money may be the root of all evil, but, by God, the thought of it keeps you going when the flesh weakens.

I duck-dived under the grill. It was a good four feet, not two, to get under it. I came up, gasping for breath and hit my head against the cutwater of the moored launch with a crack that made me swear. I had a feeling that maybe this was going to be one of those nights when everything went wrong.

I climbed up a stepway at the inner end of the boathouse and stood listening for a while to the sound of water dripping off me. Then I pushed open the small doorway and, without even the benefit of a fig leaf, went into the forbidden garden. A gleam of moonlight showed me a small gravel path running along the inside of the wall and, twenty yards up the path, a black blob which was my bundle of clothes. I hobbled towards it over the gravel and was within a couple of yards of it when another black blob appeared ten yards farther on. It was considerably bigger and I had enough moonshine grace for about ten seconds to see that it was a blob that had a pair of eyes and was covered in fur. Then it moved and with the movement came a sound which was pure, bloody-minded dog. I didn't stop for further identification. I jumped sideways into a shrubbery, saw the silvery gleam of a tree trunk and went up it, maybe not as neatly, but certainly as fast as Tarzan. The dog's jump missed my backside by about six inches. I went up another three feet to safety, scraping my buttocks to hell, and sat on a branch that dipped awkwardly beneath my weight. It was a young eucalyptus tree and hardly mature enough for the load.

Down below, what I now saw was a black Alsatian sat back on its haunches and began to give out a call for the rest of the pack to rally. A few minutes later a torch cyclopsed its way through the shrubbery and settled on me. The dog was silent, and the holder of the torch was silent, but the torch moved slowly all over me. It was like an army medical examination, no delicacy at all.

I said, 'I hope to God that's not Miss Suma Tung or anyone else of her sex.'

A man's voice said, 'Come down.'

I said, 'Not until you immobilize that dog.'

'Sarah won't touch you now,' he said.

'You've got her word for that?'

He said, 'I'll get your clothes, sir.'

The torch wandered off and then came back. I climbed down and heard him step back, well away from me, but keeping the torch on me. Beyond its glare I could see nothing. I dressed slowly because I had a lot of thinking to do. Then I said, 'You're sure about the dog?'

'Bitch,' he said. 'Yes, sir.'

'Where is she?'

'Just behind you, sir.'

The torch wavered down and past me and I turned to see Sarah on her haunches, a great flap of tongue lolling out of the corner of her mouth.

Knotting my tie, I said, 'What now?'

'Up to the house, sir,' he said. 'And keep just nicely ahead of me. Follow the gravel path. And don't think I've only got a torch.'

I said, 'Who are you?'

He said, 'I'm the butler, sir. Frost.'

I presumed it was his name, not the immediate weather

58

forecast, and I took the gravel path, following my own torch-thrown shadow along it and seeing very little until he said, 'Mind the steps, sir. Seven and then the door handle is on the right.'

'Thank you, Frost,' I said.

I found the door handle, twisted it, and went into a great pool of light, marble floor under my feet, an impression of a marble run of curving stairway on my left and a vista of three crystal chandeliers swinging low from a tall ceiling over a run of refectory table as long as a cricket pitch. Somewhere ahead there were great red velvet curtains. Old master faces looked down at me from dull gold frames, and over a radio P. J. Proby was giving hell to 'I Apologize'.

I turned and looked at Frost. He had a bland smile on his plump face, and his shirt front was starched in a way I could never get the laundry to do mine. In his non-torch hand he had an automatic. Sarah had disappeared. No dogs in the house, I imagine.

The radio was turned off, which was okay by me. A woman's voice said, 'Thank you, Frost.'

Frost gave a small inclination of his head to someone beyond me and did a U-turn through a small doorway under the marble staircase.

Suma Tung was sitting in a high-backed chair right up by the velvet curtains, and the colour of the background contrasted vividly with the black silk gown, high-necked, embroidered with golden water lilies and the odd white crane delicately scratching its nose with one claw. In one hand she had a long ivory cigarette holder with an unlit cigarette in it, and in the other she had a small transistor set which she put carefully on the table at her side. She looked like some Manchu princess, right down to little gold slippers with pearls sewn all over them, and I wondered if I should go down on my knees and whack my head in humble salutation on the marble floor. And I was also wondering what the hell I was going to say. . . .

59

But before I could speak, she said, 'You really swim naked under the boathouse grill?'

I said, 'How would you know?'

She said, 'It is the only way. Two months ago we had clever little alarm fitted to boathouse gate.'

'Harry slipped up,' I said, and I shivered.

'The whiskey,' she said, 'is over there.' She pointed the cigarette holder towards a sideboard that looked like the façade of Wells Cathedral and I started to make the pilgrimage towards it, saying, 'Just so long as it isn't whiskey brewed by anyone in the Irish Tourist Office. I've got a sophisticated palate.'

'For me,' she said, 'champagne and vodka.'

I worried at the wire round the champagne cork and she watched me in silence until it went pop.

'Is a sound I like,' she said.

'Is a sound most people like.'

I felt I was making a good show of being casual and friendly. I went over to her carrying the drinks. She took hers and then tapped the raised platform on which the chair stood with the toe of her slipper.

'You sit there.'

I squatted at her feet, like a court entertainer. For all I knew it was an accurate description. Maybe she was hoping to get a lot of fun out of me.

She drank, giving a little lift of her glass to me, and then sat in silence. I took a couple of swigs of the whiskey and felt something returning to me ... courage, perhaps. What I really wanted was a good cover story, but for the life of me I couldn't think of one. I began to wonder whether this wasn't one of those rare occasions in life where truth – or at least a fair slice of it – wasn't the best answer.

Suddenly she said, 'Well? I wait for you. Surely you begin to talk ... to explain yourself? Surely, there is very much to explain?'

I liked the way she spoke, with a gentle rise and fall, like a bird just awakened and coming up for the morning chorus.

60

'There is a lot,' I said. I fished for one of my cards and handed it to her. She looked at it and then gave it back.

'Rex,' she said. 'In Latin that means king?'

'Yes.'

'Is a nice name.'

'Thanks.'

'But does not mean you are a nice man, necessarily.'

'True.'

'So I wait to see.'

She smiled and dipped her cigarette holder towards me and I got out my lighter. Over the flame I saw that she had deep, dark eyes, just flecked with touches of yellow.

I took another instalment of whiskey and decided on partial truth.

I said, 'Do you remember seeing me at the Ascanti Club?'

'Yes – briefly.'

'I was most impressed with your singing.'

'Thank you. But you not tell me you swim here to get my autograph?'

'No. I've been employed by a firm of London solicitors to find a man called Arnold Finch. His aunt has died and left him six thousand pounds. One way and another I discovered that he had come to Ireland at the beginning of February, stayed a night at O'Toole's Hotel in Glengarriff, and then had been brought out here. I just want to find him and tell him the good news.'

I stood up and wandered away from her. I was at a disadvantage sitting at her feet.

'You could have come out in the daytime and rung the bell to make your inquiries.'

She had a point there, but I wondered if it was genuine. She sat there like a princess and her eyes never left me and they were full of something, maybe all the wisdom and mystery of the East – whatever it was, it gave them a nice lustre. For some reason she was enjoying herself.

'I could,' I said, 'But in my business one has to be discreet. Arnold Finch hadn't made any response to newspaper advertisements for him. Maybe he had some private reason for not doing so. Maybe good reasons. I like to respect people's good reasons. Just to barge bluntly in here might have embarrassed him.'

'It never could have done.'

'Why?'

'Because no man of that name ever came here.'

'No?'

'No.'

I handed her the photograph of Arnold Finch, alias Arthur Fairlawn – though I wasn't going to mention that name. She looked at it and handed it back.

'You've never seen him?'

'No.'

It could have been a lie, or it could have been the truth. Years ago I gave up trying to make that kind of decision, particularly with women.

'Then my information must be all wrong,' I said.

'I think so,' she said. And then she sat, silent, looking at me, and I had the feeling that the final summing up was being done.

Then she said, 'Why you go to the Ascanti Club? To look for this man?'

'Yes. I had a tip that he went there. I felt I might get some information about him.' I smiled. 'May I say that you're being very reasonable about all this, and I appreciate it.'

'That is a nice thing to say. But tell me, what do you do now about this man?'

'I go on looking for him ... God knows where, though.'

'I see.'

I had a feeling that she probably did.

I said, 'It's an odd world. I wouldn't be backward in coming forward if there were six thousand pounds waiting for me. But there you are ... some guys couldn't care less.'

She said, 'You like money?'

'Who doesn't?'

'You never have much?'

'Up and down. I drove around in a Rolls-Bentley the whole of one month. I was holding it against a gambling debt.'

'You gamble a lot?'

'A fair amount. Not always with money, though.'

She smiled at that and it was like the sun rising over the green paddy fields, and I was telling myself to watch it, Carver, this girl isn't making pleasant chit-chat.

'Your business ... it is always legitimate? I mean you never find little opportunities for, maybe, happy profits you never tell anyone about?'

I grinned. Happy profits.

'I'm no saint,' I said. 'But I've got certain standards. Not so high that I don't jump over them now and then. Why?'

She shrugged her shoulders. 'No reason. I am just interested in people. I like talking to you.'

'Ditto.'

'Please?'

'I like talking to you. But I think now I ought to be getting back. I apologize again for ... well, for the way I came, but in my job it doesn't always pay to be orthodox.'

'And how you get back?'

'Well ... I'm not sure.'

'Frost would not like to get the launch out at this time. Of course,' she smiled, 'you could swim.'

'If you say so. But in that case, perhaps I'd better have another whiskey to keep out the cold.'

'Please do that.'

I went and fixed another drink for myself. She had done no more than sip hers. Champagne and vodka. Billings drank that mixture, too. Turning, I found her watching me with a neat little curl of a smile on her lips.

I said, 'Is your sister here, too?'

She shook her head.

63

I raised the glass of neat whiskey to her and tipped it back.

She said, 'You are a good swimmer?'

'Medium.'

There must have been a bell on her chair somewhere which she had rung for, at this moment, Frost appeared through a door under the marble stairway.

Suma said, 'Frost will show you your room. There is everything in it.'

'Thank you,' I said. 'That's the kind of room I've always wanted.'

'Goodnight,' she said.

'Goodnight.'

I moved to Frost and he stood aside for me to go up the stairs, his plump face graven with impassivity. Nothing that happened in this house was ever going to surprise him, that was clear.

Behind me the transistor radio was switched on and from a French station a man started to read the news in a breathless way as though he had to get it all out before the world finally blew up in his face. Personally, I felt that I had a crisis on my hands too, not cosmic, but I hoped, promising.

FIVE

Gather Ye Rosebuds

SHE WAS right. The room had everything. Pyjamas, dressing-gown, shirts, some casual trousers and cardigans in a hanging cupboard, all more or less my fit. There was a bathroom off the bedroom with silver dolphin heads for taps and a cabinet full of everything from an electric razor, after-shaving lotion, through to aspirins and some cans of tomato juice and a bottle of Lea and Perrins.

The window was on the southwest side of the house, and looked right down Bantry Bay. The moon had come on for a brief shift and I could see the white horses riding in and, away to the right, the dark, craggy summits of the Caha Mountains. It was all very wild and romantic, and I wondered what was in it for me.

I got into bed, took off my Omega automatic – a present which I had bullied out of an ungrateful Swiss client who'd got himself into a mess in a Soho clip joint – and hung it over the crooked finger of a tiny ivory hand which stood on the bedside table. There was an internal telephone there, too; one of the old-fashioned kind that they charge you thirty guineas for in Harrods. I lay back and looked at the silk hangings of the four poster and thought God bless this house and all who in it lie – and I knew there wasn't a soul there, including myself, who wasn't nourishing some little bundle of falsehoods.

I must have been asleep an hour when the telephone woke me. Not right away. It had a discreet, silvery note that took some time to get through and, even when it did, I was still drugged with some nameless, shapeless dream which I had been enjoying and, now, felt I'd never catch again. I fumbled for the phone without putting the light on, found it, and said, 'Yes?'

Suma's voice said, 'I wake you?'

I said, 'Yes.'

She said, 'I am sorry. But I am in trouble. And I hate them so much. Oh ...' there was a little whooshing sound of childish fear, 'Oh, it touch me then!'

'What touch you?' I asked. She didn't sound like a woman being murdered.

'A bat. It is in my room through the open window.'

I made myself comfortable against the pillows.

'You're sure it's a bat? It's a bit early in the year for them.'

'Of course, indeed. I see it. Once it is against my hair. And in your hair, they say, you cannot get it out.'

'It's never been proven,' I said. 'Anyway, what you want is a tennis racquet.'

'A what?'

'Tennis racquet. Swipe it hard. Backhand or forehand and mind the ornaments on the mantelshelf.'

'But I don't have any racquet. Besides I am under the bed sheet.'

'Just you and the telephone?'

She said, with a little note of anger, 'You come to help me or not?'

I sat up. Some day I was going to retire with a fortune and surround myself with ordinary people who worried about mortgages and athlete's foot and who said, more or less, what they meant.

I said, 'Okay. How do I find the room of frightened Miss Suma?'

She said, 'It's next door to yours. On the right.'

I got out of bed and put on the light. There was no tennis racquet in the room which was a bit of an oversight really. The only thing I could find was a long-handled back-scrubber in the bathroom. I took it and padded out into the corridor. The room was ten yards down to the right.

66

I went in and switched on the light. It was a much bigger room than mine with a king-sized bed with a black velvet padded headboard. A flex trailed from the bedside table into the bed and the sheets were mounded up like an anthill from beneath which came Suma's voice, saying, 'It is Mr Carver?'

'It is,' I said. 'But you should have sent for Frost. He's bald and would have no fear of the bat getting into his hair.'

The room curtains were half drawn, and the window was partly open at the top. So far as I could see there was no sign of a bat – and this didn't surprise me. However, if a woman called for bat help, a man would be churlish not to respond.

I swiped at an imaginary bat and missed. But I wasn't worried. It was a long time since I'd done any bat swiping and you need a couple of swings to get loosened up. I swung again and knocked a couple of pounds worth of value off a gilt chair.

Her voice from under the sheets said, 'You have got him?'

'No,' I said quietly. I needed a little time to think.

'Be quick,' she said. 'It is difficult to breathe here.'

'I'll do my best,' I said. 'But these Irish bats are tricky.'

I did a few more swings and then I walked to the window and shut it.

'Okay,' I said. 'You can surface now.'

'You are sure?'

'Yes, indeed.'

'I am very grateful to you.'

I stood by the end of the bed, back-scrubber in hand, and watched the sheets heave.

She had the most beautiful brown shoulders and small firm breasts and she was giving me the same kind of trans-figuring smile that either she or Lian had given me for a moment in the Ascanti Club.

She said, 'You like all this light? It is so bright.'

I walked to the door switch and said, 'It wasn't the light that was making my eyes blink.'

I switched off and at the same moment she put on a subdued rose-red number at the bedside table. The turn of her arm and the movement of a naked shoulder as she moved higher in the bed were pure murder to a country boy like myself.

'Since you are here,' she said, 'perhaps we go on with our nice talk?'

I hesitated for a moment, but that was only out of politeness, then I dropped the back-scrubber and moved towards the bed.

'Don't let's rush it,' I said. 'We'll get round to the talking.'

Under the red light her bare little breasts were like twin rosebuds and as I stooped to gather them I said to myself, why not, Herrick was a Devonshire man, too?

As the grey light of a rainy dawn seeped discreetly through the half drawn curtains, I sat on the edge of the bed, feeling for my slippers, yawned, and said, 'What about this little talk?'

Behind me, she gave a long sleepy sigh, and said, Later.'

I turned and looked down at her. The whole thing, of course, could have been stage one of a beautiful friendship. That was all right by me. But beautiful friendships are rare and develop more slowly, usually. It was stage one, all right – but of what? Whatever it is, I told myself, don't rush it.

She rolled her head towards me and gave me a warm lazy smile. She reached up a long, bare arm, put it round my neck and pulled me down to her. I found myself kissing the soft hollow of her neck just under the port side of her chin.

She said, 'You like me?'

I surfaced for air briefly and said, 'Didn't I give that impression?'

She giggled and then grabbed my right wrist and held it firmly.

She said, 'You like money, too? And some excitements?'

'Some excitements, yes. And money – even if it is sometimes dishonestly come by.'

'That is good. We talk about it later. Now I go to sleep.'

She let go of my wrist, closed her eyes and went to sleep. So I went back to my room, taking the back-scrubber with me.

I shaved and bathed, dressed in borrowed casual clothes and went down and out into the garden. Sarah appeared before I'd taken four steps and we made a friendly promenade through the shrubberies in the soft rain, and I put the whole position to Sarah. Being feminine, I thought, she might have a new angle on it.

'A beautiful girl hands you the order of the oriental bed, first class, and then talks about helping you to money. And, I guess, she doesn't mean a few fivers. What would you do? If you were me, that is?'

Sarah stuck her nose into a fresh mole hill and blew through her nostrils. If there was any symbolism in it, then it escaped me.

Back in the house Frost welcomed me with a cool good morning, eyed my wet shoes with disapproval, and said would I like kippers, or eggs and bacon, or both?

I said, 'Tomato juice, one poached egg on toast and then coffee.'

Over breakfast I read a three-day-old *Irish Times* and tried to do the bridge problem. I didn't have any success with that either.

After breakfast I had a quiet wander around the inside of the house, because from the garden I'd spotted something tucked away in the middle of the roof complex which interested me. I made a fairly accurate guess of how to reach it, but decided to leave it alone until I was less likely to be disturbed.

At twelve-thirty, Suma appeared in the great hall in another of her Manchu princess dresses, gave me a cool little bow as though we were in the middle of my ambassadorial cocktail party and said she would like a glass of champagne and vodka. She sat on her throne and accepted it from me as though I were a royal cup-bearer.

She put her lips to the glass, wrinkled her nose a little as the fizz touched it, sipped, put it down, and then smiled at me. The smile was reinforced by a movement of her right hand.

In it she was holding a pistol. One way and another I've had a lot of experience with firearms, and it wasn't difficult to recognize this one. It was a Browning automatic, calibre 6.35 mm – a baby Browning. A small job, but what is it the Scots say? Guid gear aft gangs in sma' bulk, or some such thing. I wasn't much more than two yards from it. She fired it, and the bullet hit the marble paved floor a foot from me and went high-tailing away in a crazy ricochet to thump into the wall somewhere near the stair-case.

I said, 'For Christ's sake!'

She fired another shot the other side of me, and laughed as I jumped backwards. There were six cartridges in a magazine. Four to go.

She let her hand drop into her lap and looked at me. I breathed deep through my nostrils like a frightened horse, and said, 'What was all that in aid of?'

'Truth,' she said.

'You haven't done the marble floor much good.'

'It was demonstration. Marble floor is very easy cleaned of blood. Also, any body dropped in the sea here always the tide takes it out. Never comes back.'

I said, 'Was that in your house agent's particulars?'

She giggled, and then said, 'You have spilled your drink. Please . . .' She motioned to the sideboard.

I went like a homing pigeon to the gin. My mouth was a Sahara and there was something wrong with my knee

70

joints so that I had to sit down on the nearest chair to stop from buckling.

I lit a cigarette, fumbling over it as though it were the first time in my life. 'Truth's okay,' I said, 'so long as it cuts both ways.'

'Maybe.' It was a favourite word of hers. 'But you start – about Arnold Finch.' And she said it with a flick in her voice which made me wonder whether this was the girl with all the love talk of the previous night.

'Okay.' This was no time to monkey around. 'I have reason to know,' I said, 'that Arnold Finch goes under the name of Arthur Fairlawn. He's wanted for his part in a two-million-odd industrial diamond steal in London – last February. He came to this house on the 3rd February last. A day after the robbery. I'm a business man – part of my business is recovery of stolen goods. For this diamond job I might touch five per cent of the total. That's a lot of money. For that kind of money I'd take the odd chance of floating out into Bantry Bay with a bullet in my back. Maybe it's going to happen, but if it is, just let me say I couldn't have passed a more pleasant last night on earth.'

She smiled, delighted like a small child, and said, 'What a nice man you are. And different. Please–' She held out her glass to me. 'A little more vodka.'

I took it and laced up the champagne that remained in it with a fat refreshener of vodka. I handed it back to her and, as she reached for it, I slammed my left hand across her lap and knocked the Browning to the floor. I jumped for it, grabbed, and spun round.

She was still smiling at me and raised the glass to her lips.

'Good,' she said. 'I expect something like that. But check the magazine. There were only two shots and I have used them. If I wish – I just ring for Frost.'

I checked the magazine. She was dead right.

I said, 'I give up.'

She shook her head. 'No – you just begin. But first I tell you some truth. Not all the truth. Not all at once – but

71

enough. Later – if things are right, I tell you, maybe, nearly all the truth. And, if you are clever, if you help me, then you will have money. But not a hundred thousand pounds. Ten, maybe.'

'A tenth of a loaf is better than none.'

'You don't ever find these diamonds. It is too difficult. No one ever finds them. So, as you say about the loaf – it is better to get what you can. You know what are my sister and myself?'

'Two delightful girls.'

'We are both of us officials of the Ta Chung-Hua Jen-min Kung-Ho Kuo.'

'What's that?'

'It is the People's Republic of China.'

It was obvious now. Industrial diamonds. The Chinese were always in the market for them. But what had she got up her sleeve for me? No diamond reward for recovery, so she said. Well, I could always nourish that dream. In the meantime ... well, I'd always settle for ten thousand if I couldn't get fifty. Maybe I could get both, and the thought didn't make me remotely feel unashamed. It's a hard, tough world full of cracked marble floors and bodies floating seawards.

I said, 'This house belongs to your government?'

'Indirectly, yes.'

'And you and your sister are their agents?'

'Yes.'

'And you're going to buy these industrial diamonds?'

'Yes.'

'If ever I got away from here, I've only got to tell the police that.'

'So? How does it help them? Maybe they know already. But if you tell them – maybe we kill you. Anyway, you don't get any reward because the diamonds are very safely hidden – and you don't get any money from me.'

'You've got a point there. So?'

'You know the underside of London well?'

'The underworld?'

'Yes.'

'Fairly well.'

'And you are a resourceful, ambitious, not easily fright-ened man?'

'You can put that in writing for me sometime. So what next?'

'If you agree – two things. One I tell you now. The other I tell you later, when I am more certain about it.'

I said, 'All right – let's have it in instalments.'

She said, 'My sister and I – though we live much abroad – have difficulty to employ people who can be trusted. All Chinese agents have this. For governmental things abroad, discreet things, we cannot use our nationals because they are so obvious. Therefore we use other nationals. Often they are unreliable.'

'I could come in that category.'

She smiled. 'After consideration of you, I take this risk. In life there is always risk as on apple tree always some fruit with maggot inside.'

'Confucius, he say?'

'Please?'

'Never mind.'

'You understand the problem?'

'Sure, you're looking for a discreet non-Chinese na-tional?'

'Yes.'

'And was last night your usual recruiting gambit?'

'Only sometimes. It is good to mix business with pleasure. Very good. When omens are right.' She gave the briefest of smiles, and then said, 'Even without need for you governmentally, I would have been happy to call for bat help from you.'

I grinned, 'Any time. Just ring. So now, let's get back to the governmental side of the People's Republic of China and the underside of London, and the fact that you've got me fingered as someone who might like to make some money more or less dishonestly.'

And as I spoke, I was thinking, deep back, and trying

73

to sort the tangle. Billings had to be in this somewhere. He and Fairlawn were sellers. But I decided not to mention Billings's name. I was ready to bet the whole of the Yangtze rice crop against a China orange that if Wilkins had been there she would have sniffed and said, 'Get out, now. Even if you have to swim to Glengarriff.' But not me. Just at that moment I was sure, without having been told by Suma, that I had a good set of omens. And good omens mean fat bank balances if you know how to use them.

'So what do I do?' I said.

'I want a man,' she said. 'An expert. He must be discreet. I pay him well – through you – in any currency. I pay you well also for arranging him.'

'What has this man to be an expert in?'

'Diamonds. I work for my government. The industrial diamonds are important to us. I spend their money. I must be sure of the value of these diamonds.'

'You don't trust the other side?'

'A lot of money is concerned. I just must be sure that there is no hocum-pocum.'

'And this man – when do you want him and where do you want him?'

'You go to London for him?'

'Yes.' I went and sat by her chair.

'I will let you know in some days. There is no hurry.'

'That's how I like to do business – leisurely. You want to discuss the money angle now, or later?'

'Later. We shall be generous – but you and this man must be discreet.'

'Don't worry. Neither of us will want to spoil a good thing. I'll go back to London tonight.'

'No. Tomorrow is perhaps better. I like you here.'

I looked up at her, and she let a warm smile drift down towards me like a summer cloud. But she didn't fool me. Before I was allowed to leave here she was going to have a quick check carried out on me in London.

I said, 'I like you here too.' I genuinely did. But I also

liked doing myself credit with my bank manager. I was thinking that if she could afford to wear a tiny, diamond-framed wristwatch which must have set the Kung-Ho Kuo boys back quite a bit at Asprey's – then they ought to be pretty generous with me.

We had fresh salmon for lunch, no boiled hake, and the rain let up for an hour in the afternoon so we took a stroll around the garden. Then she disappeared until it was time for drinks before dinner, and I sat at her feet. After dinner – fillets of steak with a good burgundy of which I drank most – we played solitaire, or she did and I helped and kept wondering all the time why the thing was so leisurely. No hurry, no fuss . . . our business, the money side, had been settled before lunch. Now, there was all the time in the world.

I could see that in a diamond deal like this you would have to have a valuer – but it was a bit hard to swallow that, the moment I poked my nose in, it made me the ideal man to arrange one. The best way to have dealt with my intrusion would have been to have shot me and dropped me in the sea. Suma needed me for something. But what?

By eleven o'clock that night I was still wondering, but reasonably happy about it. She had chatted away without much help from me and saying nothing that made me any the wiser. The only information I got about herself was that she and Lian had been born in Shantung province and that their father had been a great friend of one Lin Piao – deputy Prime Minister and Minister of Defence – and that they had been educated in Hong Kong. No mention of her mother. Nothing else personal, except some stories of their travelling in America and Europe.

I said once, 'With an average birth rate of 37 per thousand and a death rate of 17 I can think of other things than industrial diamonds your country should buy.'

'We not talk about China politics,' she said.

'What we talk?' I said.

'We talk about you.'

'Good subject.'

'Why you always look to make quick big money?'

'Because I have a quick, big appetite for good things. All carvers like a big joint to slice.'

'Maybe you should become a vegetarian?'

'Nuts.'

She giggled and it was pure magic. It was a pity she had a job to do, and did it efficiently. I liked her just as Suma. Maybe I could have got to like her a lot. I didn't, though, have any illusions about her. She could be hard and ruthless – had to be for the job she was doing. If it had been necessary I would have been dead by now. I would have to watch my step with her. It was hard – watching her – to keep that in mind.

We talked for a while longer, and then she said she was going to bed.

She walked towards the marble stairway, turned at the bottom, flashed on a smile and said, 'You think bats are creatures of habit?'

'Irish ones, yes.'

'I was hoping that would be so.'

She turned and went up the stairs.

I fixed myself a whiskey and soda for a nightcap and sat and smoked for a while, thinking.

When the whiskey was finished, I wandered out of the great hallway into the corridor. Sarah was sitting on an old Donegal tweed jacket with leather patches on the elbows in an angle of the wall. She gave me a gentle yawn, rose and padded along with me. She had a night-watching brief and the freedom of the house.

I went into the room next to the great hallway and then slipped out just a little too fast for Sarah, shutting the door on her. I waited while she whined a little on the other side. Then she went quiet and I left her and went up to my room.

It was midnight. And bat time wasn't until about three. I had a couple of hours. I got into pyjamas, dressing-gown and soft slippers. The rain had stopped and there was a young slip of moon making a bad job of avoiding a fast

76

scud of clouds. I opened the window and climbed out on to the sill. It was not difficult. I'd checked that from the garden during the day. To the left of the window there was a six-foot run of thick, square rain piping that ran up to the gable valley to one side of my window.

I went up it, and then along the gable valley to the hinterland of a roof and turret-broken plateau. In the centre of this were three chimney blocks and up the side of one of them, stapled to the wall ran a length of rubber-coated flex. It finished at the chimney top in a short stubby aerial with a half-circle wire-basket affair which – from the ground earlier that day – had seemed unlikely to me to be either for television or just domestic radio.

In the light of the moon, I followed the flex back across the roofs. After about six yards across a leaded flat, it turned the corner of a little fanlight in the roof and disappeared through the brickwork. The fanlight was fastened down permanently and the four large squares of glass had been covered with black paint. But that had been some time ago and the paint had weathered. A little gleam of light was showing through one of the panes of glass. I rubbed at it gently with my forefinger and made the patch bigger. I put my right eye to it, and there wasn't even the beginning of a whistle of surprise in me.

The little room below was fitted up like a ship's radio cabin. There was a transmitter and receiver against one wall and Frost, headphones on, was sitting at it, tapping away on a morse key. Standing directly behind him was Suma. She was wearing a long, quilted dressing-gown, black with yellow birds over it. As I watched she pushed back the sleeve of the gown and looked at her watch. She was all right at the moment. There was quite a time to go before bat hour.

Frost stopped tapping, and then he picked up a pencil and began to write on a pad as, I presumed, a message began to come through. I could see the pad clearly, but not well enough to read what was being written, but there were about six lines of script. Then he stopped receiving, took

off his headphones, and ripped the top sheet off the pad
and handed it to Suma. She read it and then stuffed it into
the pocket of her dressing-gown. I hoped that she was
going to leave it there. Could be it was the clearance – or
otherwise – on me from London.

They stood talking for a moment or two and then they
both passed out of my sight, presumably to a door because
the lights went out.

I wandered back across the roof, slid down to my room,
and sat and smoked for a while at the window, thinking
of the diamond reward.

Half an hour later the telephone rang. I didn't bother to
answer it. I padded down the corridor to her room.

There was a pale dawn light coming through the window
when I woke. Suma was in deep sleep, flat on her back and
half uncovered. I ran a finger lightly from the hollow of
her neck, down through the valley of her breasts to the
dimple of a delicious navel. Somewhere, under the layers
of sleep, the ghost of a smile moved the corners of her
mouth. Satisfied with the reaction I slipped out of bed
and went quietly towards the window where her padded
dressing-gown lay across a chair back.

I slipped my hand into the dressing-gown pockets. Nothing. Well, she was a careful girl. I wasn't surprised. Just a
little disappointed, maybe.

SIX

Under Starter's Orders

I HAD BREAKFAST late and loafed around the garden until just before lunch and then went back to the great hall to be on time as cup-bearer for Suma.

Frost came in, carrying a silver salver, his face as ponderous as though he was deliberating devaluing the pound.

There was a letter on the salver. It read:

> I am so sorry. I have had to go unexpectedly.
> I am at the Savoy, London. Make sure your friend
> has a passport. Love. Suma.

'How did Miss Suma go?' I asked Frost.

'Lunch is ready whenever you are, sir,' he said.

'I'll finish my drink first. Perhaps you can have Harry here after lunch? I'm leaving. What time did she go?'

'Harry will be here at two-thirty, sir.'

'You're a mine of information.'

And Harry might have been, too. But I didn't try any digging as he motored me across to the pier where the Cork boats used to call.

As I went ashore, Harry unbuttoned and said, 'You had a good time, then, sir?'

'I did that, Harry.'

'Aye, I thought so, sir.'

I got in on an early plane the next morning. Coming out of Customs at the airport I thought for a moment that I caught sight of a face I had seen before among the people grouped to welcome arrivals. The crowd moved and I lost it, and I couldn't be sure that I had been right. However, I decided that it would be wise to take no chances.

I got my bag and found a taxi outside. On the way in to London I slipped the cabby a fiver and told him to drop me unobtrusively somewhere around Sloane Square and then take my bag on to Mrs Meld's and dump it with her. For once the cabby wasn't a chatty type. He just pocketed the note and nodded.

He dropped me on the north side of Sloane Square and moved away in the circle of traffic. I went across to Peter Jones and loafed for a while in the china department – which I felt was appropriate – and kept an eye on the main door. A willowy girl with black velvet eyes tried to sell me a Lalique horse without success. Nobody came through the main door who looked like the man I had thought I had seen, so I went to the telephones and called Miggs.

He arranged a meeting with me in Portland Street at the car salerooms of a friend of his. I left the telephone, got lost in the store and then, with a few apologies, went out through the goods entrance and got a taxi within three yards. When you were working for the Ta Chung-Hua boys, I decided, it was wise to take precautions. I didn't want to advertise the fact that I had become part of the Yellow Peril.

The cab dropped me some way up Portland Street and I strolled down to the saleroom and went in. Miggs was there. He was standing with a dreamy look in his eyes, stroking the nose of a type 44, straight-eight, 3-litre, 1927, touring Bugatti, coachwork by Gangloff. It was some time before he became aware of my presence.

When he did, he said, 'What the bloody hell are you playing at? I've had to stand up two gym appointments for you.'

I said, 'The Hatton Garden Diamonds – industrials. You think it was two-and-a-half million?'

'The Press exaggerates – and the people who lost them. But why?'

'I've got a buyer for them – but they have to be valued.'

He gave me a hard look, that was slowly tinged with

sympathy and said, 'So you finally went mad. Strain, I suppose.'

'I'm the buyer's agent. I want a valuer. One who can be trusted.'

'You want a strait-jacket.' He looked at the Bugatti, tapped its nose and said, 'Isn't she lovely? Why bother with women?'

I said, 'Just give me a name, or I'll write to the tax people telling 'em how you cook your accounts. The man has got to be reliable.'

He pushed his big lips out and thought and then said, 'I know one bloke – and it's his line of country. He used to be with the Diamond Corporation. One of their best valuers. Used to go around the West End wincing at all the paste stuff that some dolls were hoping would pass as real. Then, while he was still legitimate, he took up with some fancy slack and went overboard about her and needed a bundle to keep her in mink and caviare. He did three years, in the Scrubs, I think, for bilking his employers. Something about undervaluing to a customer and then taking a cut on the real value difference. He's a nice chap, but a bit dodgy if the talk ever gets round to women.'

'Who is he?'

'Don't let it put you off, but his name is Horace Goodenough. He has a flat near here. Hallam Street. Does very well for himself now. Valuing for fences and big outfits . . . international stuff some of it. Works a lot in Germany. Beirut, sometimes.'

'Think he would have any part in the original H.G. steal?'

'I know he didn't. He grumbled about it to me once. Hurt pride. Didn't like being kept out. Take my advice – you stay out too.'

'Could you ring him and say I'll be calling – right away, if he's there?'

He looked at me, then shrugged his shoulders, and said, 'You've got your head down, haven't you? Strong scent coming down the wind, tail high – and a packet of trouble ahead of you. Go back to Wilkins and be a good boy.'

'I could look him up in the directory.'

'Don't bother. Man wants to commit suicide then I'm always ready to oblige.'

He moved away from me and went to the saleroom office. I could see him through the glass partition, standing behind a blonde who was thumping away at a typewriter not only as though she hated its guts, but was determined to get at them. He was less than a minute on the phone.

He came back.

'He's there. Sydeley Mansions. Flat 10.'

I gave him a big grin and patted the nose of the Bugatti. 'Thanks. One day, maybe, I'll buy you one like this.'

He shook his head. 'Any buying, it'll be me. A big wreath for you.'

I went out the back way of the saleroom and walked unhurried to Hallam Street.

It was a cosy flat, with two Peter Scott bird paintings in the hallway. In the sitting-room Horace Goodenough went for leather upholstery and, I learned later, his own water colours. He wasn't very good at waves. Coffee was set out on a low Benares brass table, and there was a bottle of Benedictine on the tray.

Horace was a roly-poly man of about fifty, with comfortable little creases of fat above his collar, a pair of mild grey eyes and a fuzz of grey hair like the fluff you find under beds in sloppy boarding houses. He wore a black city jacket and striped city trousers, a grey waistcoat with a big silver chain across it, white starched collar above a blue shirt, and a black tie. Somehow, he didn't quite make the impression I was sure he meant to give. But he was a friendly soul.

I began to give him a card, but he waved it away.

'No need. Miggs said you might turn up.'

'He's a great friend of mine – and discreet.'

'Great virtue.'

'Would you be interested in some free travel – and a fat fee?'

'Would a drake look at a duck?'

'This Duck flew out of Hatton Garden last February.'

He gave me a chubby stare, then said, 'You want a glass or do I just put the Benedictine straight in the coffee?'

'Straight.'

'Shall do.'

As he poured the coffee, his back to me, I said, 'It was a very neat job, wasn't it?'

Without turning, he began to dope coffee with Benedictine, and said, 'It pains me every time I think about it. The thing was made for me – on the marketing end.'

'I represent the buyer.'

He brought my coffee over to me. I sipped. It was half liqueur and I coughed gently.

'You want a valuation?' he asked.

'Down to the last sixpence.'

'Careful buyer. You've come to the right man. Things have been slow. I'll lower my commission a little.'

'No commission. One thousand pounds. All expenses. Probably a week's travel abroad. Any currency you name.'

He sipped his coffee, but there was no cough, and he was looking at me hard.

'Done,' he said eventually.

'Fine. Do I have to set out the conditions?'

He sat down carefully in a big club armchair, hitched his trouser knees up with one hand and frowned.

'I know what you mean,' he said sadly. 'But you don't have to worry. I made one mistake, once, with one woman. Sticks to you for life it seems. She lives in Bromley now, two kids, husband's a bookie. When I get into a strange bed now, I put a gag on. Awkward, but you get used to it – if you're naturally a chatty man like me.'

'This buyer,' I said, 'would be very annoyed if anything went wrong.'

He did a balancing trick with cup and saucer and produced a cigarette from somewhere.

'Life used not to be so difficult.'

'This is easy – so long as you do exactly what you're told. Passport in order?'

'Yes.'

'I'll be in touch with you.'

'All right if I bring my painting things? There's often long waits.'

'These yours?' I nodded at a nuclear sunset blazing over a blue and white meringue sea.

'Just a selection. Know my real ambition?'

'I can guess. To be accepted by the Royal Academy.'

'Try every year. I'm a great tryer. Nothing ever puts me off.'

He did another balancing trick, this time with coffee and cigarette, and then the cigarette was in the corner of his mouth and his right hand was holding an automatic on me.

'What's that meant to prove?' I asked.

'That I don't like tricks either. You're all right. Miggs gave me the word on you. But just tell your client that I work, straight if he wants it that way, and then I get paid as per contract. All right?'

'Understood.'

'Splendid.'

He conjured again, clumsily, and the automatic went.

I said, 'One day you'll injure yourself with that.'

He came to the flat door with me and his parting words were, 'You know, I think sometimes that the Royal Academy isn't as traditional as some people think.'

From Horace's place, I took a taxi to the Savoy Hotel and went in through the river entrance. I went up to Suma's room, knocked, and she let me in.

She was wearing black ballet tights and a yellow blouse and her hair smelled good as I held her in my arms for a few moments.

We sat on a sofa together and I told her about Horace.

'You trust him?'

'I think he's okay. I got a good reference.' Through the open door to her bedroom I could see a couple of half-packed, open cases on the floor. 'You moving out?'

'Yes, today. Lian and I have another engagement . . .' she hesitated, and then added, '. . . in France. Lian is there already.'

I said, 'Arthur Fairlawn had a girl friend once, Bertina Brown.'

'Yes. I know her. She works for the Ascanti Club.'

'Not now. She's disappeared. When I began to make inquiries about Finch. Any ideas where she might have gone?'

She shook her head. 'About these other people I know very little. Maybe you frighten her.' Then she gave me a look and suddenly smiled. 'Oh, I see – you like her a little?'

'My interest is professional.'

She leaned forward and kissed me on the lips.

'Liar. But it does not matter. Suma is not jealous. You and I – we understand each other, no?'

'Yes.'

At the door, she said, 'About money. Already I arrange with our agents to pay you the first part. They are respectable people, so no trouble for you. From France, soon, I telephone you. And when you come over, we have plenty of time together.'

'Good.'

'Also – if you like, I find out where is this Bertina for you, no?' Her eyes were full of laughter, and before I could say anything she closed the door on me.

I went down in the lift not needing to convince myself that I had met my match. I was a convenience. Fun on the side, maybe. Her favourite word. But get no wrong ideas. She didn't care a damn about me. One wrong step and Miggs would be ordering that wreath.

I got back to the office about five, and Wilkins, full of disapproval, brought me a cup of tea in which she had deliberately put sugar knowing I didn't like it.

She handed me an opened letter with a cheque clipped to the corner of it. It was from a firm of City bankers saying

that in accordance with instructions from their clients –
Agencia Ganero, Panama City – they enclosed a cheque
for the first instalment of services. No receipt was necessary. It was for a thousand pounds and I fingered it lov-
ingly, and there was the faint howling of the wolf pack
beating a retreat down Northumberland Avenue to the
river.

Wilkins said, 'Do I get to know about this?'

I said, 'I'll give you a full summary tomorrow – and you
can lock it in the safe.'

'To be brought out on your demise?'

'My what?'

'Have you signed any contract with this Agencia What-
ever-it-is?'

'I never sign anything – but it's all in order. You should
try looking pleased.'

A tiny thundercloud had formed on her brow and the
bright blue eyes were flying storm signals.

'You can't,' she said, 'take money from Armstrong and
Pepper, and also from someone else?'

'Why not?'

She frowned. 'The simplest thing you touch in no time
at all becomes too devious for words. In a moment of crisis
where would your loyalty rest?'

'In a moment of crisis – with me. Did I ever bilk a client?'

'Once or twice.'

'Ah, but that was when I was young and learning the
business – and anyway it was deserved. Look, Arnold
Finch I find for old Lancing. What I do in my spare time is
my own business. This—' I tapped the cheque, '—is a
straightforward commercial job.'

'Really?' It wasn't just sarcasm she got into the word,
there was a nice lacing of gall and wormwood.

'Yes,' I said.

'Then it's odd, isn't it, that from this morning our office
phone has been tapped.'

I stared at her, surprised.

'How do you know that?'

She smiled, wintry but triumphant. 'Because I was told so – officially.'

I slumped back. 'Oh God – no. Not again.'

'Oh God, yes – again. So you watch your tiny little steps.'

She moved to the door, half-opened it, raised her free hand to touch her rusty hair, and then in a warmer voice said, 'There are times when you make me wonder why I stay here.'

She went out.

I reached for a cigarette, unthinkingly, and snapped my lighter at it only to find that I was trying to light the cork-tip end. Well, there was an excuse for it.

What the hell could they want? Or even, how the hell could they know?

It was the vellum-faced number from the Ascanti Club who came to my flat at ten minutes past ten that night, the fish fancier, and expert in Chinese musical instruments. I'd treated myself to a whole lobster and a green salad on the kitchen dining flap, lingering over it with the evening papers and a cheap bottle of white wine. I was flopped in my armchair watching television when he came in.

If I'd wanted any confirmation that he wasn't police, his entry would have clinched it. The police go for tradition . . . the heavy tread on the stairs, the double knock which takes the paint off the door panel, and a silence broken by a noisy clearing of the throat. This chap was one of the boys from the shady side of Whitehall.

I didn't hear the door open. He was just suddenly there standing a yard from my chair, his feet washed with the pearly light from the television screen.

I said, 'Sit down and watch this.' It was an old Laurel and Hardy film and both comics were on a roof, fixing a radio aerial. He sat down on a footstool. Stan Laurel turned, sideswiped Hardy with the end of a ladder, and the fat man slid off the roof into a lily pool.

The fish-fancier laughed and I knew then that he was too human to get very high in his profession. Laurel shuffled to the edge of the roof and looked down at Hardy and his foot dislodged a tile that caught Hardy full and square on his bowler.

I said, 'I can think of a lot of people I'd like to see this happen to.'

'Sutcliffe wants to see you,' he said.

I'd heard that summons before.

'Let him wait,' I said. 'And since you seem to be around so much, you'd better put a name to it.'

'Vickers. Edwin.'

'Who else is there?'

I leaned forward and switched off as the commercial came through with a great steamy shot of sausages and baked beans that made me feel ill.

'Casalis,' he said. 'You know him?'

'Sure.'

'Better not keep them waiting.' He sounded sad. 'They're getting you down.'

'I've been in it too long. Next year I retire. My brother owns a hotel in Scotland. I'm going to run the bar for him.'

'Nice quiet life.'

'I suppose so. Trouble is we don't get on very well.' He stood up and eased towards the door. I reached down and felt for my shoes which I'd taken off.

I said, 'You really know about Chinese musical instruments?'

He shook his head. 'Encyclopaedia Britannica.'

'What about fish? Those *tanichthys albanastes*, for instance.'

'*Albonubes*,' he corrected. 'They're white cloud mountain minnows and they come from China.' He looked at me, dead pan.

'Why,' I said, as I stood up, 'should there be all this steam up on your side of the road about a few diamonds?'

He still gave me the familiar security look, dead face, dull eyes and a slight turn-down of the mouth. It wasn't difficult for him because his face was more or less that way naturally.

It was a black saloon, parked outside Mrs Meld's front

door, and it was driven by a man with a thick neck who took us through the traffic with a sturdy indifference for other people's rights and the sure knowledge that any policeman who flagged him would get a flea in his ear.

We swung into Covent Garden at a rate of knots, scattered a few people just coming out of the Royal Opera House, crushed a long string sack of brussels sprouts, and then I was decanted at the door of Sutcliffe's flat which most people would have taken for the entrance to some seedy publisher's offices, and the car was gone.

I'd been there before, several times. Always this flat. They don't ask you to call at their offices. Sometimes I wondered if they were quite sure where their offices were or even whether they had any. Hackett, Sutcliffe's manservant, opened the door to me and looked surprised which didn't fool me. He'd taken a good look at me over the monitor before he'd opened the door.

He said, 'Nice to see you, Mr Carver. Putting on a bit of weight?'

'Too many potatoes. Can't afford meat. If I'm not down in fifteen minutes send up a glass of bicarbonate.'

He turned down his mouth and said, ' 'E's in no mood for flippin' flippancy.'

He never was. I went up on my own and couldn't stop myself giving a little tug to my tie before I went in.

There were two of them there. Casalis and Sutcliffe.

I caught Casalis's eye and he winked quickly. I liked him. He was one of Sutcliffe's Paris men, and I'd worked with him before. They had a habit of hauling me in from time to time and putting the harness on – but only if I had something special to offer them. One way and another, of course, they were as ruthless as I knew Suma could be if it suited them. And this, of course, had to be something to do with Suma. Casalis was a youthful-looking forty, a shade overblown, fair hair, honest brown eyes, and was in a much higher security service bracket than poor old Ed Vickers would ever be. And he still got a kick out of the

whole business. Must have appealed to the eternal boy in
him.

'Nice to see you, Carver,' Sutcliffe said.

'You're the last person I wanted to see,' I said.

He grinned. He was lying back in an armchair, a floppy
old corduroy dressing-gown wrapped loosely around him,
and his neat little feet were up on a small stool. He was a
plumpish number, dumpy, and wearing dress clothes under
his gown. He had a smoking cap on, and somehow he re-
minded me of Queen Victoria, latish period.

'Sit down,' he said. 'And don't give us any sauce.'

'You usually offer me a whiskey,' I said.

'Running true to form,' said Casalis.

'Later,' said Sutcliffe. 'If you deserve it.'

I lit a cigarette and stared at one of the modern paintings
on the wall. It looked like a long vegetable marrow with a
couple of triangular breasts and a squashed watch for a
navel.

Sutcliffe said, 'You've been to Ireland. Why?'

'On a job,' I said.

'Specify,' he said.

'I'm trying to trace a bloke – for Armstrong and Pepper,
Solicitors – who doesn't seem too keen to pick up an inheritance of six thousand pounds. Name of Arnold Finch.'
I knew with him that you had to be careful what you picked
to leave out because you never knew what he knew. He
seemed satisfied.

'Where in Ireland?'

'Hotel in Kenmare and—'

'Don't be a buffoon!' Cold steel whistled through the air,
each word double-edged.

'Did I say something wrong?'

Sutcliffe shifted his feet on the stool, and began to pack a
pipe.

He said, 'I want the full story.'

'So do I,' I said. 'I want to find Arnold Finch and collect a fifty quid fee.'

'Where did you go in Ireland?'

'Kenmare,' I said. 'I had a lot of money running on my horse and I wanted to protect it.'

Sutcliffe smiled, and said, 'And did you enjoy your midnight swim?'

The bastard. He always had one up his sleeve. I put a good face on it, grinned, and said, 'So Harry is one of your boys. Well, he fooled me, be Jasus.' Just below my feet was a lot of deep water, but I made up my mind then that I wasn't going to jump. I would have to be pushed.

Sutcliffe said, 'If the Chinese People's Republic keep a country house in Ireland – which they are quite entitled to do – we like to have someone handy. Now give us your story, straight. By the way, I think I should tell you that we know you visited a certain flat in Hallam Street today, and that you also called on a Miss Suma Tung at the Savoy. And I'll be honest – at the moment I have no idea why. But I'm going to know, of course. One way or the other.'

And I knew what that meant. If it wasn't one way – then it was the other down in the basement with Hackett performing and the bright lights going. Thank God, I'd so far only known about this by hearsay.

I said, 'I want to see my lawyer.'

They both smiled, and Sutcliffe said to Casalis, 'Give him a whiskey.'

Casalis took his time, and everyone relished the silence except me. The whiskey, as always, was Glen Livet. I took it gratefully, sipped and thought. Trade, I decided, was the best solution.

I said, trying to make it dignified, 'You've got your ethics, and I've got mine. If you want a confidence from me – then I'm entitled to one from you.'

'You're entitled to nothing,' said Sutcliffe.

I twiddled my thumbs and looked mute of malice.

Casalis said, 'Perhaps a little give and take?'

Sutcliffe cocked an eye at him. 'You think so?'

Casalis nodded. 'He knows how to keep his mouth shut and I've found in the past that he responds to kindness.'

'That's me,' I said. 'And when have I ever let you down?'

'Not recently,' said Sutcliffe. He looked at Casalis and said, 'Fill him in.'

Casalis lit a cigarette and scratched the top of his head.

'Suma and Lian Tung are Chinese agents. They've been around a long time. Efficient – and both poison. They're listed in most countries' intelligence files.'

'Nice act they've got, too.'

'So Vickers says. They also confine themselves mostly to one branch of work.'

'Which,' said Sutcliffe, 'I'm sure that even you, bastard as you are, wouldn't approve of.'

'Shock me,' I said. I couldn't see that illicit diamond buying would.

But he shocked me all right.

'Chinese chief product,' said Sutcliffe.

'After rice,' said Casalis. 'Opium, heroin, snow, horse, dream stuff, poppy juice.'

'What?'

'We shocked him,' said Sutcliffe.

And, by God, they had. I had a quick picture of all the junkies and the hopheads, and the teenagers just hooked and stealing to buy a shot . . . a kind of Hieronymus Bosch nightmare, of the whole twitching, lying, fornicating, murdering, do-anything-to-get-it thousands all over the place.

'They're the European end,' said Casalis. 'For the last two years the stuff has been coming in faster than ever before. So much so that it isn't just any Bureau of Narcotics job alone. It's security. These two nice little Chinese misses with their sing-songey banjo and tinkle-tinkle lute are the top operators. It makes a fat currency haul for the Chinese Government – and they need foreign currency because, for reasons that need not bother you, they're buying gold like hell . . .'

'He looks a bit sick,' said Sutcliffe.

I finished my whiskey in one go.

'I thought he was tough,' said Casalis. 'But there's always something that gets the toughest of us.'

He was right. I was sick. I had had a friend once who just never could get to level off until he took an automatic to himself.

Sutcliffe said, 'They've got this all organized very sweetly. A few lines of entry we know. So now, tell us why you take a midnight swim out to Gowduff Island?'

I got up and helped myself to another whiskey. Neither of them said anything. Everything was very still so that the soda hissing into the glass sounded like Niagara.

I stood there, looking down at the bubbles of soda winking out, and I was telling myself that the odd step or two over the white line was one thing, that just now and then you could harness up a couple of half-truths to a rickety wagon and drive home with a harvest load you'd done nothing to sow or work. Now and again ... yes. But not always. Like the good book says, there's a time for everything and, although it was against my nature normally, I decided that this was a time for truth – and, if necessary, to kiss the cash goodbye.

I went over and sat down, and still they said nothing. Sutcliffe blew a cloud of pipe smoke and disappeared behind it like a squid.

I said, stupidly, 'You're dead certain of this?'

Casalis nodded.

'All right, I'll give you everything.'

'Everything?' It was Sutcliffe.

'Yes.'

So I did. I gave them the whole thing from the moment Wilkins had dropped *The Times* on my desk until the moment that afternoon when she had told me that our telephone was tapped, and they heard me out without interruption.

I finished, 'I guessed you were coming into this when Wilkins said she'd been informed the phone was tapped. Why'd you do that?'

'We had an idea you might be useful to us. If you know your phone is tapped you don't waste your time handing out lies to us. We don't like wasted time.' It was Sutcliffe.

I said, 'Do you think Billings is at the top of this pile?'

Sutcliffe said, 'We don't know. This is a new angle. I'll have to speak to the Yard about it. But one thing is clear – the Chinese people aren't going to waste currency buying industrials. They'll do a straight trade for drugs of equivalent value.'

'But what about me?' I was recovering a little. You have to if you want to go on enjoying life. 'Do I walk out of here with a nice big thank you, or is someone going to make out a temporary employment card for me in some Ministry?'

Sutcliffe smiled. 'You ought to be slung in clink for accepting employment from Suma Tung. But that's a detail. Sometime in the future those drugs – if we're right about that – have to be exchanged for the diamonds. We'd like to be there. You're already *persona grata* with Miss Tung, and she says she's got something else up her sleeve for you. So you carry on.'

'What about terms?'

Casalis said, 'He recovers from shock fast.'

With a touch of anger, I said, 'Get this straight – I'd like to bitch this thing up, too. But I'm a working man. I haven't stuck any insurance stamps on Wilkins's card for months.'

Sutcliffe stood up.

He said, 'You get the usual fees from us. You get whatever you manage to get out of Miss Tung. And if the diamonds are recovered you get your percentage of the reward – which means that you'll be arguing with the loss adjusters, or whoever they are, for months. Casalis is assigned to you. He or someone else will be right on your tail all the time.'

I said, 'And how far do I go?'

'As far as you can. Make yourself useful to Suma Tung. She's taken a fancy to you, hasn't she?'

Casalis said, 'You'll have him blushing in a minute.'

Sutcliffe said comfortingly, 'You'll get your instructions when to bail out.'

I said, 'Once every two years you do this to me.'

'Once every two or three years—' he said, without concern, '—you do it to yourself.'

I said, 'Horace carries water-colour paints and a rather old-fashioned automatic. I have hand luggage, too. Do we get a clearance on that if we have to travel?'

'Naturally.'

'And if I'm up against a wall in a bad light with something dark making for me?'

'You get a clearance for that, too. Naturally. But try and avoid it. You want a list of the other things to avoid?'

'It's a long time since you went over them.'

'Avoid temptation – money, women and fast dealing.'

SEVEN

Dressed to Kill

AT NINE o'clock the next morning the telephone rang.

It was my friend from the Yard who had given me a clearance on Arnold Finch.

He said, 'Hullo, sunshine – did I wake you up?'

'No.'

'Well, never mind, somebody's going to.' I could hear the bubble of contentment and happiness in his voice. 'Old friend of yours.'

'Who?'

'Deputy Commander Barnes, OBE, MC, C Division.'

'Oh, no.'

'Oh, yes. You're to report to his flat. Queen's Gate – you know it.'

I did, and him.

I said, 'Why there?'

He chuckled and it was like a hen giving thanks for the safe delivery of a double-yoked number. 'Because,' he said, 'he's laid up with gout, and he was kept up very late last night – and I don't have to tell you who by. Get cracking.'

Gout – and last night he'd probably had the whole diamond case taken out of his hands by Sutcliffe! And he was within a few months of retiring and he'd probably seen the cracking of the diamond case as a chance to go out in a real blaze of glory. He was a lot of things; efficient and a hard worker, but he was also a great one for glory. And he had a temper like a volcano coming apart at the seams. And he hated my guts because once or twice I'd helped him in an unorthodox way and made a little on the side which – for policy reasons – he had had to overlook. Anyway, he didn't like my kind.

On the way there, the taxi-driver gave me a run down on what to do in the garden this week, and said that any man who didn't like gardening lacked some essential human quality.

I said, 'I'm going to see one now.'

He was in his sitting-room wearing a velvet smoking jacket, wide open to show a crumpled expanse of shirt over a chest as big as a herring barrel. He had red, close-cropped hair, and eyes a little darker blue than those of the Siamese cat he nursed on his lap. He was a great monolith of a man, hewn from red sandstone. His right foot in a loose bed sock was propped up on a stool. On the wall behind him were some signed photographs of boxers and cricketers, and there was a racing oar right across the top of the mantelpiece. If it had been allowed he would have hung the scalps of criminals there, too.

His first words were, 'Don't come near my bloody foot.'

I sat down a good four yards away.

'Nice to see you again, Commander,' I said.

'Don't talk crap. You know what's happened. This diamond thing's been more or less taken out of my hands. Security.' He made it sound like a dirty word, which perhaps it was. 'But I'll be fair – I'm not blaming you.'

'Thank you.'

'But I'm bloody well warning you. Any monkeying around from you and I'll have your tripes.'

If anything his language, I thought, had got even more colourful.

I said, 'I'm not likely to monkey around. I'm in the hot seat.'

'I don't care a damn where you are. There's just one thing I'm interested in – the boys who pulled this steal. Security or not – I'm going to have them.'

'That's very laudable.'

'Don't be bloody flippant.' His big voice came rumbling from his chest like Vesuvius snoring.

'So why am I here?' I asked. 'You've got all the information.'

I lit a cigarette without asking his permission and it was at this point that the cat jumped off his lap and sauntered like a long-legged fashion model across to me and started to sharpen her claws against my thigh. I'd known a few real models that did that, too – so, I hoiked her away with my spare toe, gently. Barnes, I could see, didn't like that either.

In a voice, modulated to distant thunder, he said, 'You make out a complete statement! Everything – go down to the Yard and do it! And don't make any mistake about the Bertina Brown woman's part. Get that right. The straw-headed bitch! She knew all the time that Fairlawn had a cover as Finch. If she'd come across with that when we questioned her we might have picked him up. It could have been the one thing that might have closed everything up for them. If I get my hands on her, she'll get a couple of years at least.'

Right then I cursed myself that I hadn't thought of this when I had spilled everything to Sutcliffe. I didn't think she could have had much to do with the diamond steal. I could guess how she came to be on the fringes. But this Finch-Fairlawn thing nailed her. And it was I who had presented Barnes with it, through Sutcliffe.

I said, 'She probably didn't know what was involved. Just helping an old boy friend without—'

He used one graffiti-like word. I didn't try any further justification.

'You make the deposition. That's all I want. And then you can bugger off and play boy scouts with that Whitehall crowd. Get me?'

I nodded.

'Good, that's all.'

I stood up and moved for the door. Before I reached it, he said, 'You've worked for Sutcliffe before?'

'Yes.'

'Christ – they must be hard up.'

At this moment the cat came and did that twining manoeuvre between my legs.

'The police aren't all that particular either at times,' I said. 'It's the age we live in.'

'All right. I'm not trying to ride you. I just don't like you. Though,' he looked down at the cat, and, maybe it was his idea of mollifying me for being beyond his pale, said '—she seems to.'

So I went down to the Yard, and I wrote it all out, and everyone there was in a good mood, even expansive, so that they told me although they were sure that Billings was in the diamond job they'd be lucky to ever get to pin it on him. He was so far at the back that there was always the risk of getting jungle-bound and dying of starvation before he could be reached. I didn't care much. I was thinking of Bertina. She was in trouble and I was the one who had pointed it her way.

Coming out of the Yard, I found a pub and had three large whiskeys, went without lunch, and finally reached my flat still wondering what else I could have done but hand over the truth to Sutcliffe.

Suma called long distance at six o'clock in the morning. I came out of sleep, fast and clear-headed. She was brief and gave her instructions clearly, and I was glad about that because, apart from the fact that I knew the conversation was being monitored, I realized that this new drug angle was going to take me a while to absorb before I could start playing any affectionate gambits. I would have to, some time soon, because the act would have to be kept up. Well . . . we're all surprised at times at the things we can do if we have to.

When she had rung off, I lay back and went to sleep. Casalis woke me at half past eight. Mrs Meld, who was doing her morning chores for me, let him in. I could hear her banging around between the sitting-room and the kitchen singing *Star of Eve* in her Guinnessy voice and obviously full of joie de vivre.

From the door, Casalis said, 'Maria Callas outside wants to know whether it is two eggs or one?'

'Two,' I said. 'Three if you're joining me. And the bacon just on the curl. But she knows.'

He went out and came back with a couple of glasses of orange juice.

He raised his glass. 'Top of the morning to you lover-boy.'

He was wearing his all's-right-with-the-world smile, and a purple-and-green-checked jacket. Both were horrible. He straddled a chair, nursing his orange juice, and said, 'Suma called, I understand.'

I said, 'Don't you blokes ever sleep?'

'Like babes,' he said, 'once a year on holiday,' and added, 'Is she always like that?'

'Who? Suma?'

'No. Mrs Whatsit outside.'

I said, 'You've got *Lover Come Back to Me*, and either *Bye Bye Blackbird* or *Take a Pair of Sparkling Eyes* to face before we get the eggs. And talking of food, what's the Hôtel du Golf, Divonne-les-Bains like?'

'Posh, comfortable, first-class service, over a hundred rooms, but I'd advise you to eat at *Le Marquis* – wonderful *truite au bleu*. You can fly your car direct from Lydd to Geneva and then it's only a few miles motoring back over the border into France.'

'I haven't got a car.'

'You're not up-to-date. It's outside. You have a booking for two o'clock tomorrow afternoon. I understand she said there was no mad hurry?'

I said, 'I'll have to organize Horace.'

'Do that.'

'And I suppose the next time I see you you'll be dressed up as a French charcoal burner?'

'I haven't decided yet. Like to wait for the moment of inspiration.'

I struggled up in bed, swallowed the orange juice, lit a cigarette, and then looking him full in his clear boyish eyes, I said, 'What happened to Bertina Brown? Is she still in this country?'

He considered this and finished his orange juice. Then he said, 'We went to work on it yesterday. France, some days ago. Regular route. Train. Two nights in Paris – and then into thin air. Hoping to meet up again?'

'It's too early in the morning for hopes. How long have you boys had tabs on Suma and Lian?'

'Since they were about seventeen. You'll never see it, of course, but their dossier is quite something. Mixture of Sax Rohmer and Peyton Place. They're both poison.'

At this moment Mrs Meld's head came round the door and she sang 'Pack up all your cares and woes' at me, winked, and said, 'Breakfast up, Mr Carver, and that electric coffee-grinder's gone phut again so I made you some nice Nescafé.' She went out on the wings of song and I could hear her clear down the stairs and out into the street.

I said, 'You've got to have a snow-white conscience, and not a nerve in your body, to be as bright as that so early.'

I struggled into a dressing-gown and went out to breakfast. I picked up the *Daily Mail*, had a look at Fred Bassett and Flook and over the top edge I said, 'You think the drugs come in on this *SS Dahlman*?'

'Could be – but they're probably unloaded a few miles out at sea.'

'What's Sutcliffe's angle? Wait until drugs and diamonds meet – then jump?'

'Could be. Everyone, and everything in one bag. Then keep it quiet, so that he can bargain.'

'With the Chinese?'

'Why not? He'll probably trade the girls back against something he wants. Anyway, the drug thing will be killed – for the time.'

'Barnes won't be happy if there is no publicity.'

'Oh, we'll let him have that over the diamonds so that he can notch up his convictions.'

I poured a second cup of coffee and said, 'I could end up with my throat cut – long before I get to any point where I could help you.'

He smiled. 'That's what gives life its zest.'

'You and Mrs Meld.'

At the door, wiping egg yolk from the corner of his mouth before going, he said, 'You'll get an official visitor at the Hôtel du Golf. Aristide the name is. Treat him nicely. He'll just be making his number, and he'll give you some instructions. Thanks for the breakfast. See you sometime.'

I watched him, from the window, walk away to the corner by the river. He was having trouble to avoid bouncing.

Against the pavement was a dark blue Ford Zephyr 6, saloon, registration number 30KP. On my breakfast table lay the keys.

I lit a cigarette and called Horace Goodenough.

I said, 'I'm picking you up at eleven tomorrow morning, full marching order. All right?'

'Where are we going?'

'All I can promise you is a few nice sunsets over the water.'

An hour later I was in the office, facing Wilkins and giving her the whole story – except for a few small details which I knew would shock her.

When I had finished, she stood up and began to leave the room.

I said, 'Aren't you going to say anything?'

'Like what?'

'Oh, good luck. Or England's destiny couldn't be in safer hands?'

'Good luck,' she said and then, opening the door, added, 'I'll bring you in some cheques to sign before you go.'

I said, 'I could be killed.'

'If you are,' she said, 'I'll let your sister know, and I'll put an announcement in *The Times*.'

Good old Wilkins, efficient to the end.

I picked Horace up just before mid-day and we drove down through Kent to Lydd. Horace wore a very neatly pressed seersucker suit, black and white co-respondent shoes, a panama hat with a ribbon of what might have been his old school colours around it, and he had an enormous old-fashioned brown case with him, the leather on it rubbed bare like the hide of some diseased buffalo. He didn't say much on the drive down. At the airport he loaded himself up with newspapers and magazines, and a packet of wrapped barley sugar and went through Customs control with the look of a doomed man. On the plane he pulled his safety belt tight enough to give him hernia and kept his eyes shut until we were well airborne.

'I can see you're mad about air travel,' I said.

He shook his head. 'It's unnatural. Always goes straight to my guts. When I was in the trade I always insisted on going by sea. Sierra Leone I did, twice a year. Lovely trip. Wonderful sunsets.'

We were in Geneva by four and, while Horace didn't exactly kiss the soil when we got out of the plane, I could see that he was glad to have the trip over.

I bought myself a Michelin map at the airport – Sheet 70, Beaune-Evian – and we drove the eight or nine miles north to Divonne-les-Bains which was just over the French border. It was a nice little town with the Jura Mountains running north-east behind it, and a talkative trout stream skirting the edge of the park in which stood the Hôtel du Golf and the Casino. Somewhere, distantly, up the hill near the golf course was the sound of cowbells.

The Hôtel du Golf was an enormous place full of thick carpets and quiet service, and I had a room on the fourth floor. There was a balcony that looked straight out over the flat country to Lac Leman and, if the sky had been clear, I could have seen Mont Blanc. Down below, on the hotel terrace, was a large swimming-pool. Looking towards the lake, Horace's room was on the right of mine, and to the left was Suma's room. The hotel reception clerk had handed me a note from her when I had checked in with Horace.

It read:

> Welcome. I am away until about seven-thirty.
> See you for drinks before dinner in my room (115).
> Suma.

Her balcony was only about three feet away from mine, and I could see that the large french window into her room was open. It was only three feet. Nothing really. Except for the long drop to the terrace below. Two women were sun-bathing by the pool. A handful of children were splashing in the water and an old gardener in a blue apron was raking the gravel. There was a fair chance that he might have some extra raking to do soon, but I took it. I said to myself, 'Just imagine you're doing this six feet above ground level and not sixty, and it's easy.'

I made it and took a large patch of skin off my right hand. I stood on her balcony and looked down to see if anyone had noticed from below. The scene had not changed. The gardener raked, the children splashed and shouted, and the two women went on quietly burning.

The lay-out of her room was exactly the same as mine; a big bedroom with a desk and a table, a row of glass-fronted hanging cupboards, and to the left of the little passageway that led to the main door a bathroom and then a lavatory. I wasn't worried about what I was doing. I had two employers now, and I had to serve them equally well.

There was a book by her bedside with a marker in it. I picked it up. It was called *Les Blondes Ont La Vie Dure* by somebody called *Martin Meroy*. I opened it at the marked page and the first paragraph read: 'Quelque chose, en cette jeune femme, m'excitait plus que je n'osai me l'avouer . . .'

That sounded like a line from any man's autobiography. And it went on: 'Tandis que je la regardais, non sans plaisir, moulée par les draps légers, elle se redressa, demasquant ses épaules nues.'

Well, my French was good enough not to lose any of that and I made a note to borrow the book later. But at the moment I was more interested in the slip of paper which I had seen projecting from the top edge of the book. It's odd what people use as book markers, pound notes, income tax reminders, paper clips, a dried stalk of corn. This was a cablegram folded longways in three.

It read:

ARDENNES E 19 GROGNON
LA FAUVETTE

It was from the Agencia Ganero in Panama City and addressed to Suma at the hotel. It didn't have the feeling of a code message – but then that's how the best code messages should be. I put the book and cable back.

There was a large empty suitcase at the bottom of the wardrobe cupboard. All her stuff was put out neatly on shelves and you could tell by the way it was done and the stuff that was there that she was an experienced traveller.

She had a crocodile leather case with gold and tortoise-shell fittings, and the scent she used was Givenchy's *L'Interdit*.

I let myself out of her room by the door into the hotel corridor and pulled it locked behind me.

Back in my room, I found a man standing on my balcony, looking down at the women sunbathing below. I went out and stood alongside him and looked down. He half turned and gave me a warm smile from a craggy, pock-marked face that had a fringe of rusty brown moustache below a hooked nose with a couple of blinky eyes above it. He was about four foot six high, and for a moment might easily have been mistaken for a small brown owl, an impression aided by a shabby brown suit, buttoned at the neck without a tie, and big brown shoes that turned up at the toes.

In English which was very good but made it clear that he was French, he said, 'The brunette with the yellow bikini is the mistress of a Swiss manufacturer of tourist postcards, views of Mont Blanc, Château de Chillon, and so on. She has two children, not his, who live with her mother in Fribourg. On the side she speculates in currency and, I have no doubt, will be in trouble again very soon. Aristide Marchissy la Dole – my name. But just use the Aristide. The rest is all faded glory from my landowning ancestors in the fifteenth century.'

105

I said, 'For all I know you could be anyone. She's got nice hips but not as good as the blonde beside her. What would *le fichier central* have on her?'

He screwed his head round in the way owls do without turning anything else and winked and said, 'You know something of the *Sûreté Nationale*?'

I said, 'In my time I've even been an *individu à surveiller*.'

'Your accent,' he said, 'is terrible. But I like your approach.' He looked down at the blonde and said sadly, 'They are always together. Some years ago – when I worked in *Renseignements Généraux* – she gave me a little trouble. But nothing could be proven against her. And neither of them, monsieur, have anything to do with this present case.'

'And what office are you in now?'

'*Office Central des Stupéfiants* – straight from the *Rue des Saussaies*.'

'Narcotics?'

'Yes. If you look to the far end of the pool, monsieur, you will see a man sitting in a deck chair under what I think you call a monkey-puzzle tree.'

I did and there was. And although he was wearing sunglasses, a basque beret, and was naked except for rust-red summer trousers, I saw that it was Casalis.

'So,' I said.

'It is Monsieur Casalis, monsieur. When I raise my hand to him, he will take off his beret. He is watching us.'

He raised his hand and Casalis casually took off his beret.

'Content?' Aristide screwed his head round again.

'Content,' I said wearily. It always made me feel weary when they went through this elaborate ritual.

Aristide said, catching the end of my sigh, 'It has the appearance of useless melodrama but in some cases it is highly effective. We should go inside, perhaps?'

We went inside and I telephoned the desk for whiskey and Perrier water.

I said, 'You know the full story?'

He nodded, 'Of course.'

'Is Lian here with Suma?'

'Yes. She also stays in this hotel. Both of them are appearing in the Casino night-club, next door.'

'So?'

He blinked at me as though the daylight were too much for his eyes and said, 'If at any time you cannot contact Casalis, then you will probably be able to contact me. If you are in difficulty, just pick up the nearest phone and say to the operator *"Police Judiciaire. Rouge-sous-rouge."* You will be put through to someone who will immediately give you every assistance.'

'I can't wait for that not to work.'

'It will work for the next three weeks. And now perhaps you will give me your findings on Miss Suma Tung's room.' He pulled a shabby notebook out and began to go through his pockets for a pencil. I handed him my biro and at this moment the whiskey and Perrier came in, tray-borne, in charge of a *femme de chambre* with a nice figure. When she had gone and I had fixed the drinks, Perrier without whiskey for Aristide, I said, 'Don't tell me you haven't been through her room yet?'

'No, monsieur. And now you have saved us the trouble.'

I gave him an accurate description of all I had observed. When he had finished his notes, I said, 'What do you make of the cable?'

He said, 'Nothing. I'm just a post office at the moment.'

I shook my head sadly, 'And I thought at last I'd met someone who was going to trust me.'

He blinked his eyes. 'I mean, monsieur, nothing of significance. Ardennes, you know E 19 – to me it means nothing. Grognon. It could be a person's name. *La Fauvette* . . . well, in English that is the name of a bird. I think . . . a kind of warbler. Now you know as much as I do.'

He handed me back my biro, and went on, 'Remember you can easily get in touch by picking up a telephone.'

I said, 'You make it sound so bloody easy.'

He smiled. 'It is for the time being. It is only as time goes on that it may become difficult.'

He finished his Perrier water and stood up.

I said, 'Is that all?'

He drifted towards the door, paused, shook himself a little as though he were settling his feathers in trim for an evening flight to check the vole population and then gave a wise nod and was gone.

I had another whiskey while I showered and then called Horace on the house phone and told him that if I hadn't surfaced before eight-thirty, he should have dinner by himself. After that he was to be either in his room or the Casino next door so that I could find him if necessary.

Suma called me to her room at seven-thirty. I went in. Lian was there, too, and to begin with that made it very difficult. They were standing together near the window, both of them bare-headed, both of them in rather simple little dresses, with a touch of some white stuff at the cuffs and throat, both looked charming, demure, and so cool that butter wouldn't have melted in their mouths – and I'm damned if I knew which was which.

I said, 'This kind of situation could be difficult unless you start wearing name tabs.'

One of them came forward, reached up and kissed me lightly on the cheek.

'Suma?'

She nodded. 'Yes – and this is my sister Lian. She knows all about you.' She took me by the arm and I went over and gave Lian a little bow. I could see she was very amused. I might have been, too – in fact, I had to act as though I were – but just at that moment it was hard not to be thinking of other things ... of the merchandise that these two unloaded on an eager market.

'Which,' I asked, 'would be the older of you two?'

'Suma,' said Lian. I knew it was Lian, because Suma was the one holding my arm still.

'By five minutes,' said Suma.

'Close finish.'

'You like him?' Suma asked Lian.

'He is nice,' said Lian.

I felt I was being paraded round the ring.

There were drinks on the table and Suma went to them and began to fiddle with bottles and glasses. Over her shoulder she said, 'This Mr Goodenough is here?'

'Yes. You want to see him?'

'Not now. Maybe tomorrow. Anyway, it is not good that we be seen all together.'

'Outside this room,' said Lian, 'we do not know one another.'

Suma brought me a whiskey. 'This Mr Goodenough I want to see once, but it is better that we deal with you and give you all the instructions you need.'

'You're the boss.'

'Oh, yes – she is very much the boss,' said Lian. She had sat down in a chair by the window. There was a flash of light from the dying sun over her dark hair and below her short dress a moving sheen on the long run of her nylons.

I said, 'Then let's talk business. What about the valuation? Is it to be done here?'

'No.' This was Suma. She had settled on the end of the bed. I sat down by the table.

'Where?'

'Away from here. Some way. It is a condition from the other side. You and this Mr Goodenough must not know where you go for the valuation. So we arrange it that way.'

'That's reasonable. But how is it arranged?'

'Very simple,' said Lian. 'Sometime in the next four or five days a man comes up to you . . . in the street, maybe, anywhere, and you do what he says.'

'How will I know this man?'

'He say a word to you. Special word.'

'What word?'

From the bed, Suma said, 'Chartreuse.'

'And then?'

'You do exactly as he says.'

'And Horace Goodenough?'

'This man come to you only when he is with you.'

'Are you going to be at the valuation?'

Suma nodded her head. 'Yes. Both of us.'

She lay back on the bed, putting her hands behind her head, and her little breasts were tight against the fabric of her dress. It was hard to imagine that she and her sister were what they were. And I knew myself too well not to be deceived into thinking that I would always be able to keep it in mind. The human animal forgets easily at times.

I said, 'And the payment for these diamonds? Does that take place immediately after the valuation?'

'No . . . we have to collect the money.'

Lian stood up and came by me towards the door, a little drift of perfume moved with her.

At the door, she gave me a smile, and said, 'You come tonight and watch us at the Casino?'

I nodded.

She went out, and Suma lay on the bed and stared at the ceiling.

After a moment, I said, 'What's on your mind?'

Her eyes came back to me, and she said, 'Lian. We quarrel about you.'

'Why?'

'How can we know to trust you, she asks?'

I smiled. 'How can you know to trust anyone? Particularly in this kind of business. The best way is to make the money good – and hope. Don't you trust me?'

'Yes.'

'Then there is no problem.'

It was the understatement of the year.

'No problem,' she said.

She smiled and reached up for me. However, after one kiss, she pushed me gently away and said that she was going to have an hour's sleep before dinner and her work at the Casino that night. So I went back to my room, shaved, showered and changed, and then picked up the phone. I asked to be put through to the police and when I was, I said, '*Rouge-sous-rouge*'. In fact I said it three times before the franc dropped and then, in thirty seconds, I was speaking to Aristide Marchissy La Dole and passing him all the information I had.

He only made one comment, and that about the code word, *Chartreuse*.

'Code words are always interesting,' he said.

'Why?'

'Because people think they pick them at random. That is the object. But always – because the brain or the sub-conscious mind must be logical, no matter how far removed from truth – then there is an association of ideas.'

'You mean this guy likes liqueurs?'

'Could be.'

'It's a great lead. You've only got to sort through all the drinkers in France.'

I met Arnold Finch, alias Arthur Fairlawn, that night.

Late, after dinner in the hotel, I strolled round the corner to the Casino. In the night-club I groped my way through the gloom to a wall table, ordered myself half a bottle of wine and sat and watched the cabaret turns.

Suma and Lian did the same act, except that Suma's solo number which had tightened up my emotional strings in London was changed for a French number which – because of my scrappy vocabulary – only came over to me in odd lines. But I gathered it was the same idea, lovers with no-where to go but the Seine side, and the frustration of boy and girl who haven't the price of a hotel room. Knowing all I did know, it did not make the same impact on me.

Afterwards I went into the gaming room and played *boule*, which is nothing like as exciting as tiddly-winks, and I made myself fifty francs. On the other side of the table Arthur Fairlawn must have lost about the same amount.

I recognized him at once. He was tall with smooth, blond hair, going just a little silvery above the ears. His face was a little more lined than the photograph had shown, but they

111

were good, firm character lines; a pleasant, manly, intelligent face, charming and self-possessed. On a con man it would have been worth two thousand quid of anyone's money as a start. He was wearing a dinner jacket, smoking a cigar, and made little jokes in French with the croupiers who seemed to know him well. He looked straight at me once and I might have been part of the decorations.

But five minutes after I'd cashed my chips and gone into the bar for a drink, he came and sat down beside me.

'Carver?'

'How did you know?'

He fished in his pocket and handed me a postcard-sized photograph. It was a nice one of me, standing in the window of the hall at Gowduff with the sunlight winking off a glass I held in my hand. Frost must have taken it. I handed it back.

'Where did you get it?'

'Suma had it taken for identification purposes.'

'Clever Suma.'

'You can say that again.'

I said, 'Should you be out in the open like this?'

'Why not? There's nothing against Arnold Finch – so long as you keep your mouth shut.'

'Which I'm being paid to do, among other things.'

'So there you are. But shut really means shut – from now on until—'

'—the cortège winds its way to the grave.'

He grinned. 'That's it. And here's to a long life.'

He raised the drink he had brought with him from the bar.

I drank with him. Why not, either way it was going to be my funeral.

He said, 'You did some good leg work from Cadilly on.'

I said, 'Blame – or praise – Aunt Jessie. She was a great girl for ashtrays.'

'God, those things! I could have opened a shop with the stuff she gave me. She had a thing about Greece. Charming old girl.'

112

'She would have been proud of you.'

He laughed. 'Why not? I've made my own way in the world.'

I said, 'What about the inheritance? Even with the bundle you're nursing – six thousand quid is six thousand quid.'

'When this thing's all over I'll do something about it.'

'Like what? Make a declaration of identity in front of some notary public in Haiti and then get it shipped out?'

'Something like that, old boy. Not your worry anyway.'

'That's true.' I sipped my drink and casually gave him the big question. 'What,' I said, 'became of Bertina Brown?'

'Oh, she's around. When you started to ferret around we thought it best to get her out of the way. It turns out now, of course, that there was no need for it.'

'She's in France?'

'Yes.' He gave me an amused look. 'You don't have to worry about her welfare. You were, weren't you?'

'In a way. She's a nice girl.'

'The nicest. But not really my type – we both soon realized that.'

'She covered you well when I went to see her. It wasn't her fault that I rumbled you.' You never knew when a good character reference might not help a friend.

'Loyalty. That's Bertina. One quality you must have in a woman.'

'Did she know about the diamonds from the beginning?'

'Don't be crazy, old boy. She does now, though.'

'Don't you mind that you'll never make it back to England?'

'So what?' He spread his well manicured, strong brown hands. 'So long as you have money, and a valid passport, the world is open. Who wants England?'

'Considering the climate, I don't know.'

He stood up. 'If you see me around again, just pretend

113

I'm not there. And anyway, nothing's going to happen for a few days so I should enjoy yourself. But don't forget—' his voice dropped and he was looking hard at me, and, for the first time, I noticed that his eyes were just a shade too close-set and his mouth suddenly had a mean, narrow line to it; '—you owe us loyalty, too. And, Carver, we know how to keep people loyal.'

I smiled. I said, 'Don't worry. I'm young – and I have everything to live for.'

'Keep it that way, old boy. Too much trouble in the world as it is.'

He went. I lit a cigarette, and sat thinking. He thought he was going to make a packet out of this deal. He thought that he had everything to live for. Far away places, just one page after another of the travel brochure, and when his legs got tired – a luxury villa with bougainvillea and hibiscus over the loggia, and some woman at his side to make it all seem like home. But I was the nigger in the wood pile. And just at the moment there was a large log sticking into my back because, while I didn't mind if he did a long stretch at Parkhurst or the Moor, I didn't see anything like that for Bertina . . . or rather I *could* see it, didn't like it, and was wondering how it could be avoided that blood-thirsty old Barnes didn't get his hands on her. I smoked two cigarettes and still hadn't come up with an answer. It was easier in the old days when they hoisted you heavy with armour into the saddle, put a lance in your hand, and pointed you at the dragon. On the way out, I looked into the gaming room. Arthur Fairlawn was there, playing, and alongside him was one of the Chinese girls. I presumed it was Lian – largely, I suppose, because he had an arm round her waist as he played and from the way she kept looking up at him. If two people have a thing for one another and it comes across in public so clearly then it must be a thing with a capital T.

At nine o'clock the next morning, as I was shaving, the phone rang. It was Casalis.

'What's new?' he asked.

114

I told him about Arthur Fairlawn. It was no surprise to him. I said, 'I just thought I could smell some trouble between Suma and Lian. Any instructions?'

'No. Just play it off the cuff, old boy. Off the cuff. No one better than you for that.'

He rang off, and I rubbed after-shave lotion on my face and yawned at myself in the mirror. Then, it being a fine morning, I got hold of Horace and we walked the few yards up the hill to the golf course, carrying his painting equipment between us. I gave him the Chartreuse information. He just nodded.

'Chartreuse mean anything to you?'

He nodded. 'It's a colour – very difficult to mix. I use it sometimes for foliage effects.'

I hired some clubs from *monsieur le professeur,* and left Horace on the terrace, setting himself up to do a painting of the town in the foreground and a distant view of the lake and Mont Blanc. Horace was in a good mood. The weather was just right for his co-respondent shoes and seersucker suit.

I played around in a lazy fashion, giving myself nice fat preferred lies and allowing myself all putts up to four feet so that I knew I must certainly break eighty.

But I never knew how I would have finished. After I had played the seventh hole I crossed a road which cut right across the course and went to the eighth tee. It was a long hole, dog-legged slightly to the left with an approach shot over a boisterous trout stream to an elevated green. This stream ran all the way down the left-hand side of the fairway and, for the first two hundred yards, was hidden by a thick belt of trees. I hooked my drive close to the rough by the trees and as I walked down to the spot, a man came out of the trees. He was a tall man in blue overalls and wearing a beret and, just for a moment as I approached him, I wondered if it could be Casalis, amusing himself with a disguise.

But this man was taller and broader with a rough, weatherbeaten face, and the brown hand he was holding

115

out held three golf balls which he was clearly offering for sale.

I said, 'Non, merci, monsieur.'

I took an iron from the light bag I was carrying and prepared to clout the ball. It was a beautiful morning, all sunshine and warmth, with the trout stream in the trees making water music and the comforting scream of a jet somewhere up in the hazy blue. I took up my stance and had the feeling that I was going to hit a beauty.

Instead, I got hit. It was a hard slam with the edge of one of his soup-plate hands and it nearly took my head off. I went forward, collapsing like a rotten tree trunk. For a while there wasn't an ounce of fight and very little comprehension in me. I was like a stunned pig ready for processing, and he began to process quickly. He grabbed me by the slack of my shirt and slung me into the cover of the trees. He sat on my back and jerked both my hands behind me and tied them, quick and fast, making a little hissing noise between his teeth as he did so. He was an expert and he had it all worked out, and there were a dozen other places on the course which I had passed already where he could have gone through the same performance.

As he finished binding my wrists, I began to revive and tried to throw him from me. He cracked me again across the back of the neck. Blue flecks darted across my eyes and my mouth was suddenly full of pine needles.

His weight went from me. I was hauled a couple of yards and suddenly my head and neck were in the ice cold water of the stream, and one of his big hands had my hair and held me down. We used to do it – voluntarily – in the school wash basins. Stick your head in and see how long you could stay there without breathing. I forget what the record was. All I remembered was that I had never come anywhere near it. And I knew now, as I thrashed about with my legs and heaved with my shoulders, that it couldn't take long before the last, bubbling sigh of Carver resigning this life would go floating away down stream among the trout and the caddis grubs, flashing over little falls, swirling round in dark green pools . . . and suddenly, I couldn't wait for it. The water made a black roaring sound in my ears and I decided that it was better to swallow than to burst.

When I came to, I was lying face down, one cheek cradled on my arm, and a pair of hands were pumping away at my back. It was a nice soothing rhythm and I rode with it for a while, grunting now and then and making goldfish motions with my mouth. I began to breathe more easily. Then I was getting rid of a lot of trout stream.

The hands stopped pumping at my back. I was rolled over to face the brave new world into which I had passed. Only it was the same scruffy old world. Aristide was squatting on his hunkers alongside of me, sweating like a stevedore, with the droopy butt of a Gauloise stuck in the corner of his mouth.

He said, 'Better?'

I nodded, and winced. The back of my neck was stiff and sore.

'You were foolish to allow it to happen,' he said.

I sat up carefully.

He handed me a cigarette and held a lighter for me. I drew the smoke in deep and let it get right down into the works to dry them out.

I said, 'Where is he?'

'He saw me coming and ran. Back up to the tee you'd come from. There was a car on the road there waiting for him. I decided it was wiser to attend to you.'

'Thanks.'

'It is a pleasure.'

'Why,' I said, 'would anyone want to pull a stunt like this?'

He shrugged his shoulders.

'It's an old trick. They were testing you. They can't take anyone on trust. If you were a police plant they wanted to see if you had a cover who would come to your help.'

'And you did.'

'Only at the last moment. And I didn't show any gun.

Just that.' He nodded at a fly-rod lying in the grass at my side. 'Just a fisherman who happened by.'

'I don't like this.'

'I know,' he said. 'But you must learn to live with it.'

'You'd been behind me all the way?'

'On and off.'

'There was no car on the road when I went on to the tee.'

'It arrived as you started to walk down the fairway. I was in the trees, coming down the stream.'

'You saw it well?'

'Yes.'

I gave him a sour look. 'Yes is an answer. But I want more than that. What kind of car, make and number, and what kind of man was driving it?'

He said, 'It was a Lancia. Flavia Saloon.'

I said, 'I've always wanted one of those, but I've never had two-and-a-half thousand quid to spare. Number?'

'I couldn't get it. The bushes by the roadside hid it.'

'And the man driving it?'

'It was a woman.'

'No kidding?'

'No kidding.'

I stood up and moved into a patch of sunlight to give my shirt a chance to dry off at the shoulders.

'Nationality?'

'I couldn't tell. I could only see the back of her head. She had a white hat on, straw, kind of what, I think, you call a boater is it not, for the river?'

'She's a woman who dresses for the occasion, isn't she. A boater for a drowning party. She's really with it – and by God I'd like to meet her and that guy with gorilla hands. Any more?'

'No more,' he said.

He smiled, and began to walk away down the stream through the trees.

I went back to the clubhouse by myself and joined

Horace on the terrace. I had a large brandy and eased my damp shirt off my shoulders a little.

Horace said, 'It seems a crazy game to play in this hot weather if it makes you sweat so much.'

I said irritably, 'So what? There are plenty of streams to cool off in. I'm the active sort. You're the artist.'

'That's right,' said Horace. 'But I'm having trouble. There's something wrong with the perspective of the hotel.' He nodded at his painting.

It was the usual blue starch and foamy meringue mixture with the bulk of the hotel in the foreground done in custard yellow.

I said, 'It's not the perspective. It's the foundations. The whole thing is going to collapse any minute.'

He looked at me, hurt, but said nothing. I took a big pull at the brandy and, in my mind, went over the clothes I had seen in Suma's wardrobe. There had been no straw boater amongst them. I wondered if Lian owned one. I don't like girls who get dressed up just to kill.

EIGHT

Chartreuse for Two

THAT EVENING I was ordered to bring Horace for drinks to Suma's room. Horace, in his sedate way, was enchanted with her, and they had an animated conversation about Chinese ink-and-brush work and the scroll paintings of some dynasty or the other. I was quite surprised at Horace's erudition. After the social chat was over, Suma said to him, 'You are a very honest man. I read it in your eyes.'

'As the day is long,' said Horace, and he was on his feet before me with a light for her cigarette.

'You give strict valuation, Horace?'

'Scrupulous, dear lady, for you.'

The use of his name had brought on a Cheshire-cat smile into which he had almost disappeared.

When Horace, after a few more gallantries, had gone, I said to her, 'Take a good look at my eyes and tell me what you read there.'

She was puzzled for a moment. Then she smiled and began to move towards the drinks which were set out on a small table. 'Somebody, maybe, who needs a drink?'

'More than that,' I said. 'Somebody who doesn't like monkey tricks.' I let my voice sound angry and she turned from the table and gave me a long, inquiring look.

She said, 'What are you talking about?'

I said, 'Somebody tried to drown me on the golf course this morning.'

'Drown?'

'In a trout stream.'

'I don't understand.'

'Then, if you don't, Lian does. It must be one of you.'

'Maybe,' she said, 'you will explain.' She sounded very up stage.

'Some thug tried to do it. Lucky for me, a fisherman type came by and upset the attempt. And I can tell you this, I had hell's own trouble with my rescuer afterwards. He wanted me to go to the police and lay a complaint. Couldn't understand why I didn't want to. But I got rid of him in the end. Now, you tell me which of you two set up that stupid boy-scout test.'

'Why you say test?'

I made an angry noise in my throat and went over to the table.

'Look,' I said, 'I'm a professional man. I know my own business. And I know the ins and outs of trusting and not trusting people. Somebody wanted to know whether I was working on my own for you, completely trustworthy – or was I, perhaps, playing a double game, being covered all the time by some police shadow to look after me. Now then, let's have it – which of you is it that doesn't trust me? Or if it's both of you – just pay me what you owe me and let me get out. I don't like double games. I want to work with people who take one look at my eyes and know that I'm an honest man.'

Quietly to myself I had to admit I was doing it well, a nice blend of anger and reasonableness. Maybe the stage had missed something in me.

I tipped Perrier water into my whiskey and waited for her. She was half turned to the table, a small knife poised over a lemon which she was about to slice into her drink.

'What makes you think it has to be Lian or me?'

'The man who helped me said this thug went off in a car driven by a woman wearing a fancy straw-hat affair. Who would want to check me but you or Lian?'

She nodded her head slowly and her face was very serious.

'It is true. There could be no one else. And it must be Lian. Me, I trust you. But Lian – she not know you like

121

me. And she is suspicious of everybody. I remember, too, she has a hat like that. I will speak to her.'

'Big deal. She gets off with just a polite reprimand.'

She looked hard at me then, and I saw that her eyes had gone angry.

'When I speak to her, there will be nothing polite. You are right to be angry. You want, perhaps, that she should come and apologize to you?'

'I want,' I said, 'that she lays off any more monkey tricks.'

'This, I promise. So please say no more about it.'

She was angry, not with me I knew, but with Lian. She turned to the table and began to slice the lemon, but she couldn't have been watching what she was doing carefully for she suddenly made an exclamation and dropped the knife. She held up her left hand and I saw blood on the ball of her thumb.

It seemed a good way to end the interview. From then on I was fishing in her dressing case for sticking plaster, and showing an appropriate tenderness and concern over a cut that wasn't deep, though it was about an inch long.

Back in my own room, I wondered how far she had accepted my honest show of indignation. Completely I hoped – for my own sake. Of one thing there was no doubt. She had been angry with Lian and, I guessed, it probably wasn't for the first time. I remembered Lian saying that Suma was the boss. Perhaps Lian didn't like that and at times liked to make her own decisions.

At mid-day the next day I found a small parcel in my room. Inside was a gold cigarette lighter with a card saying, With love from Suma. I was glad that she had put the inscription on a card and not the lighter – otherwise it would have taken twenty per cent off the price when I came to sell it. But it was a nice gesture – and that, after all, is what counts with ordinary people.

That night, as it happened, in the Casino I had a wild streak of luck at *boule* – and if you want to win anything at *boule* you have to have just that. So, with my winnings, the next morning I motored into Geneva and bought a return present for her. It was a gold cigarette holder, and she was delighted with it when I presented her with it.

'I use it always,' she said. 'And always it will remind me of you.'

Well, maybe it would – but if things went Sutcliffe's way they wouldn't be kindly thoughts.

The next day Horace and I walked up the hill for a pre-lunch drink at the Golf Club.

As we were walking down the hill a dark blue van drew up alongside Horace and myself. When the driver leaned out of the cab I thought he was going to ask us the way. Instead, he flashed me a warm, chubby smile which showed off a gold tooth to advantage and said, 'Chartreuse, monsieur?'

'And the same to you,' I said.

'Hop in. Both of you in the front.'

Horace and I climbed in beside him. It was a tight fit because he and Horace were about the same girth.

We went up past the golf course and out along the road to Gex and I saw him cocking an eye at the driving mirror on the wing from time to time.

'Anyone following?' I asked.

He gave me his chubby smile. 'No. Did you expect anyone?'

'It's an uncertain world.'

'But full of good things, monsieur.'

He spoke English well but the French accent was there. I said, 'We've no pyjamas or washing gear.'

'All will be provided, monsieur.'

I said, 'If it is an uncertain world – somebody might have spotted your number plates.'

He said, 'I can see you are the worrying type, monsieur. They are false.'

Ten miles beyond Gex, heading south all the time, he pulled up.

'From here, messieurs, it is better if you travel in the back. Just a safety precaution. I have put some sacks in

123

there with straw in them. Just be careful of your cigarette ends.'

We went docilely into the back and were locked in. The van drove on.

I said to Horace, 'Is it usually like this?'

Horace said, 'It varies. Always some childish arrangement.' He lit a cigarette and stretched out on two sacks after removing his shoes for comfort. There was no peephole forward into the driving cab, no chink of light from the closed doors. We were carried along in a cocoon of blackness. And it lasted a long time, so long that Horace slept and snored.

Only one thing of interest occurred during the drive. After about two hours the van stopped, remained stationary for about five minutes, and then drove on again.

An hour later – so the luminous hands of my watch told me, the van stopped again. I heard footsteps outside and then the doors were opened. But not by the man who had picked us up. The halt had been for a change of driver. This was a much younger man, slim, wearing a suède windbreaker, pale lavender trousers, ankle-length black boots, and a smile that said he didn't give a tinker's damn for either of us.

He said, 'Please be good enough to follow me.' He had a lightish kind of voice, the sort that can go petulant very quickly. He was good looking in an epicene way, with big, baby-pouting lips.

We were in a brick-built garage, outer doors already shut. There was a small door at the back of the place. The light came from a couple of unshaded bulbs in the roof.

As the young man turned away to the door, I saw the slight bulge of a gun above his left hip.

We went out of the garage and along a windowless corridor through what could have been the servants' quarters. He pushed back a big oak door and stood aside for us to enter.

It was a big baronial hallway with a minstrels' gallery at one end. All the lower windows had their curtains drawn,

124

the light coming through a set of higher windows at gallery level. The first thing to catch my eye was Bertina Brown.

She was standing by a table which was spread with a cold buffet. She was wearing a red summer dress and a shaft of light from one of the upper windows just touched her hair, and she looked as good to me as she had ever done. But as I went up to her there wasn't much of a welcoming smile on her face. She just looked at me and gave a slight nod.

The young man said, 'As soon as you've had something to eat and drink, I'll take you down for the valuation. The rest are waiting.'

As Horace headed for the table, I said to her, 'Well . . . fancy meeting you here. Big surprise.'

'Not to me,' she said. 'Hasler told me you were coming.'

'Hasler?'

The young man said, 'That's me. And this isn't a social party. There's work to be done.' From the way he said it I had a feeling that there wasn't anything in this world which would make him like me very much.

Bertina said, 'Do you want coffee or a drink?'

'Coffee, and a nice big smile.'

I got the coffee and we all stood around as though it were a gloomy after-funeral snack where people could hardly wait to get decently away. The only person quite unaffected was Horace. There was work ahead and he was preparing for it.

His face beaming over his plate, he said to her, 'This pâté is delicious. From your own fair hands?'

'Out of a tin,' she said.

'Try the coffee,' I said. 'She makes very good coffee.'

She just looked at me, and I didn't get it. She either was genuinely pipped with me, or she was putting on an act for Hasler. I decided to say no more. You couldn't get back into a woman's favour with people like Hasler and Horace around.

Hasler gave us ten minutes flat and then we were ushered

out through another door, and along an interior passageway at the end of which a flight of stone steps ran down to a basement door. It was quite a door, steel, with heavy bolts on the outside. At the moment it was partly open and the sound of voices came through it. We went in, Horace, Hasler and I. Bertina had been left upstairs.

For the first few seconds I was trying to remember where I'd seen something like it before, and then it came back to me. Once, with my sister, I had visited some ducal castle, both of us handing over our half-crowns to support a tottering aristocracy, and we'd ended up in the long underground run of kitchens, laundries and bakeries.

The walls were faced with white tiles. Down one wall was a long row of stone basins fed by taps from a pipe that ran back to the far corner where there was a boiler affair that looked as though it could have driven the *Queen Mary*. The floor was red quarry tile with drain holes every few yards in a gully down the middle. Over the gully was a low table made of about four long slabs of marble and supported on equally spaced brick plinths. There were a lot of cobwebs in the corners of the ceilings and on the wall opposite the one with the basins, two long slits of window, high up, heavily barred, and giving a fine view of a healthy growth of nettles and docks.

In the room were Suma and Lian, and Arthur Fairlawn and Ryder Billings. Billings gave me a heavy, imperious nod and it was clear that he did not expect me to show any surprise at his presence.

Fairlawn flashed me a smile, said, 'Good trip, old man?' didn't wait for an answer and jerked a finger at the chairs which Horace and I were to sit on. Both Suma and Lian gave little oriental inclinations of the head and little half smiles of welcome, and I wouldn't have known which was which except for the fact that Suma still had sticking plaster on her left thumb.

On the table in front of Horace's chair was his small equipment case. He put a hand on it caressingly, and smiled at the two sisters.

Suma said, 'I brought it from your room.'

'Thank you, dear lady.'

So, after a few suitable murmurs from everyone, the trade delegates from either side took their places. Ryder Billings was flanked by Hasler and Fairlawn. On the opposite side of the table were Horace, myself, and then Suma and Lian, two very neat figures in blue suits.

Before him on the table, Billings had a slim leather suitcase on which his big white hands rested gently as though it were some bird which might take wing. I kept feeling that in a moment he was going to open it and read the will. In fact I had a lot of feelings but the chief one was that of all the people there Horace and myself were the only ones who were not classed as parties of the first or second part. We were merely selling our services in a negotiation of great delicacy. And that meant – you have to face these things – that once the negotiations were complete we might for security reasons become expendable. It was a seat I'd sat in before, but I was worried about Horace. He was a nice old gent about to do an honest job of work and I felt responsible for him.

It was at this point that Billings – who had been making a little speech about the discomfort of our quarters, the need for secrecy, and everyone would understand that a rendezvous like this was better to remain unidentifiable, for some, in the interests of the security of all, and so on and so on, like some Minister of State explaining policy to his departmental chiefs, and all the time his big Nero head needing no fillet of laurel to make it clear that he wore the purple and the gods help anyone who tried anything funny – said:

'So, now, let us get the business details straight.' He tapped the case firmly. 'Here are the diamonds and Suma and myself are agreed to accept the valuation put on them by Mr Goodenough. Correct?'

He looked at Suma and she just inclined her head, and very demurely she did it. But if he were a Roman Emperor who had temporarily swopped his toga for a Savile Row charcoal grey, two-button, lounge suit, she was a Chinese princess in a Dior number who still knew as much as he did about royal commands, plus all the old Manchu recipes for poison cups.

'The valuation agreed,' said Billings, 'then drugs to the equivalent value, that is to say the value as shipped at Hong Kong, will be delivered to me at a time and place to be notified within the next week, the delivery not to be later than two weeks from today. Correct?'

'Correct,' said Suma.

'No one,' I said, 'ever mentioned anything about drugs to me.'

'You know now,' said Lian, and there was a little edge in her voice.

'What kind of drugs?'

'Opium and heroin. But this hardly concerns you, Mr Carver.'

This was Billings giving me a ponderous brush off.

'True,' I said, making it sound apologetic.

Billings said, 'After the valuation here, we will have this case sealed, your seal and my seal, and it will be handed over at the delivery point, examined, and the deal so completed.'

'That is agreeable,' said Suma.

You'd have thought they really were at a conference table doing a trade for machine parts against rice, instead of stolen industrials against opium at Hong Kong prices which meant that if Horace valued at a million then Billings was going to get a cargo which, delivered in France, would be worth three times, maybe more, than that. You had to hand it to him. Why should he sell for cash? And poppy juice was like water in China so why should they waste any of their foreign currency which was gold to them? Both sides here were on to a good thing. Both were happy. And it is nice for people to be happy – but not the people the Narcotic Squads all over the world have to deal with.

I sat there, looking very businesslike, because all the

128

others were, and just for once I didn't hate Sutcliffe too much for pulling me into this. And I made myself a promise – that if I had to break a leg I'd see that the Tung girls didn't get their diamonds and Billings didn't get his Chinese cargo.

I came out of an unaccustomed spin of honest indignation to hear Billings saying:

'When this transaction is over, both parties satisfied, and the various participants dispersed, Suma and I have agreed that any subsequent breach of security by any member here present shall be a matter of mutual concern and action.' He smiled and his head turned a little towards me, 'The Chinese Republic does not want to have to make official denials of any kind about illegal drug trading. So there will be no indiscretions.' His head moved again, his eyes resting for a moment on Horace, and then he looked briefly to either side of him, passing the injunction to Hasler and Fairlawn.

And after that Horace got down to it. The case was opened and the valuation began. But don't run away with the idea that the moment the contents of the case were spilled on to the table it turned the place into Ali Baba's cave. There was no sudden sparkle of light to hurt the eyes. The case held about two hundred envelopes, each about the size of a cigarette package. Most of them had trade names on them, different names, and on the face each one carried a typed code indication.

The only equipment Horace had was a small pair of diamond scales for weighing the bulk carat value of each package, and one of those eye-piece things that jewellers use when you're trying to sell your mother's gold ring because there's a horse in the two-thirty that you must get a monkey on.

He had a pencil, too, and a pad and, as he went carefully through the envelopes, tipping tiny little piles of what looked like coffee sugar on to a glass tray in front of him, he made a note on his pad for each envelope. It was boring work and took a long time.

After about an hour Hasler disappeared and came back with a tray of coffee. Horace didn't take any. Neither did Fairlawn. He just sat across the table from Horace and kept his eye on him the whole time, to make sure I suppose that he didn't slip the odd packet into his pocket.

I went over to the far window with my coffee. Billings came up behind me and offered me a cigarette from a silver case.

I took one and said, 'Congratulations on the deal.'

'I am pleased with it,' he said.

'You should be. You'll make at least three times the value of the diamonds out of it.'

'Why not? I have a lot of people still to pay off.'

I said, 'Going to distribute yourself?'

He shook his head. 'I shall break it down into lots and sell to various agents in France. You are happy with the Tung girls?'

'No complaints.'

'Sometime, when something else comes up, maybe I can have first claim on your services? You impress me.'

It was damned condescending but it was sincere.

'I should have thought that this little killing would have satisfied you for the rest of your life.'

He smiled gravely and shook his head. 'I would be a fool to say that I didn't care about money. But I care also for action, for arranging and organizing.'

I said, 'You could always try the Bank of England or the Crown Jewels.'

He smiled, but I knew that it was only half a joke to him. Big men always nurse big dreams.

'If I ever do, Carver,' he said, 'I'll put you on the pay roll. And by the way, I owe you an apology.'

'What for?'

'The way you were handled in the Ascanti Club. If I'd known what kind of man you were I would never have been so crude. And if I'd known that you were eventually going to be working for Suma I would certainly never have had Bertina brought here.'

'You deprived me of some pleasant company.'

'But not for long. I want you to take her away from here with you.'

'What?'

'Oh, it's all right,' he said quickly. 'I know that Suma has some more work for you to do, but she has no objection. Frankly I don't want her in this house. I can't keep her locked up in a room all the time. She's a nice enough girl, and was never really involved in this affair directly. The less she knows the better.'

'She must know enough already to interest the police.'

'Quite. And I respect and trust her loyalty towards me. But one must always remember that accidents can happen. If, unhappily, things did go wrong, then the less she knows the less she can be forced to tell. You will appreciate that I am thinking of her as much as myself.'

I didn't openly dispute that. He was the big father figure, wanting to do his best for the innocent girl who had got herself all mixed up.

He went on, 'In the next few days, I'm going to have potential buyers coming here. I have their security to consider. I don't want Bertina around. She might see these men, hear things . . . all this adds up to a risk I don't want to take.'

I said, 'And what's Bertina's reaction?'

'She quite understands. Your work won't take you long and then she can go back to London. But I don't want her in London until this crucial period is over.'

Neither did I. The moment Bertina showed up at the London Airport Customs counter then Barnes would grab her. And that was the last thing I wanted. I wanted room and time to manoeuvre so that I could find a way out for Bertina.

'Fair enough,' I said.

'Good. In an affair of this kind the only factors that count are loyalty and as complete security as one can possibly arrange for the safety of all concerned.'

I suppose I should have said Amen. Instead I was

131

thinking of the reception I'd had from Bertina. She might be obediently doing what Billings wanted – but clearly she didn't regard it as any pleasure. And, anyway, somewhere trickling up my spine was a faint current of uneasiness.

Maybe, he sensed it. He put out a heavy hand and gave me an avuncular pat on the shoulder, and one of his comforting senatorial smiles. And that was that.

The newspapers at the time of the robbery had talked about a two-and-a-half-million-pound job. No doubt the insurance companies had faced, and were still arguing about, claims that totalled somewhere around that amount. Everyone should have deep sympathy with insurance companies, for the whole frail world is against them. A live coal pops out on to a piece of drugget worth a couple of quid, and dad is after the insurance company for the price of a new Hamadan. You scrape your mudguard against the garage door and, if you've got any sensible kind of human frailty at all, you try to work the insurance company for a complete re-spray job.

Horace's valuation was a few hundreds over a million pounds.

It didn't seem to worry Billings at all. He accepted it in the manner of a man who has already had his own private valuation done and knows that he is not being cheated. The diamonds were packed back into the suitcase and the Peking and Ascanti Club seals were put on it.

Horace and I were taken back into the main hall by Hasler. The others disappeared into some other part of the house.

Hasler took his duties seriously. Bertina was not in the hall, but the table of drinks was. Reluctantly Hasler allowed us time for refreshment after labour. He then led us into a smaller hall and up a flight of stairs to a thick oak door. Beyond it was a stone-flagged corridor with doors opening off it. Horace and I had adjoining bedrooms.

Before Hasler left me in mine, he said, 'Goodenough

will be going off early in the morning on his own. You and Miss Brown follow later.'

He went back along the corridor. I gave him a few minutes to get clear and then I went back to the big oak door. It was locked. Coming back I went into Horace's room. It was a small room, exactly the same as mine, with a bed, a chair, a washbasin. We had been provided with pyjamas, electric razor and the various odds and ends we would need for the night. Horace was lying on his bed smoking and staring at the ceiling.

I said, 'Well?'

He said, 'Just over a million. Never believe what the papers say.'

I said, 'We're not going to get much social life here.'

'There never is. Cagey. They always are. You do your job, get paid and get out – fast. Frankly I'm surprised we're staying overnight.'

'Maybe Hasler likes having us.'

He turned his head to me, screwed up his eyes as though he were contemplating beginning a portrait, admiring my fine bone structure. 'I've heard of him. In my book, he's strictly from the dark side of the moon.'

'Poet as well as painter.'

He went back to contemplating the ceiling. 'Just at the moment,' he said musingly. 'I'm trying to decide where to go when I leave here. Rome for a few months, I think.'

'Plenty of scope for water colours there.'

Back in my room, I flicked on the light and went to the window. Four feet away the light from my room illuminated a blank brick wall. Maximum security. It was a big house undoubtedly, and probably deep in the country. And Billings had things well organized. His buyers were on their way. Once he had the drugs it wouldn't take him more than two or three days to get rid of them.

I turned away from the window and dropped on to the bed. I smoked and stared at the ceiling, and I began to muse. It was an exercise I took often. Cheap hotel rooms were the best place for it.

Even down in the basement during the valuation it had been plain to me from various little looks and movements that Fairlawn and Lian were great and good friends. Fairlawn could never go back to England again. He'd probably got his new life all set up and waited only for his money. But wherever he went it would break up his friendship with Lian. But I didn't suppose that either of them were the kind to suffer long from heartbreak. Billings was all right. He could go back to London and nobody would have a thing on him ... I smiled to myself. There would have been a great deal more than heartbreak among them down below if they could have know about nigger-in-the-wood-pile Carver ... Loyalty and maximum security for everyone concerned. Now, there was a brace of Christian principles that would bear some thinking about ... I did, very hard.

But ten minutes later I was interrupted by the sound of the heavy door at the end of the corridor opening. Then I heard voices in Horace's room.

A few moments later Suma came into my room. I rolled to a sitting position on the bed and she sat on the chair opposite me.

I saw at once that she was in her Manchu princess mood. She said, 'I have paid Horace.'

'Good.'

She fished out the gold holder I had given her, and I lit a cigarette for her.

She gave a little smile of thanks, but didn't hold it for long. Her mind clearly was full of business. So was mine, but as she crossed one leg over the other, my interest faded for a moment. I didn't like this drug business, but the movement of nicely shaped legs brings an automatic response. Even so, as far as I was concerned, I just wanted to keep our relations from now on strictly business ones – and I hoped it wasn't going to be too difficult.

'Mr Billings has spoken to you about this girl Bertina?'

'Yes.'

I got the little brief smile again.

'I thought you liked her.'

'So I do,' I said guardedly.

'It is only for a few days. Until we can deliver the drugs to Mr Billings.' She smiled and this time held it much longer and put out a hand and touched my knee. 'And you need not think that I shall be jealous. You and me – that was very nice. But we do not make up any fairy stories about it. When we have work to do – then it is just work.'

Her hand left my knee. I had a nice sense of relief which I was careful not to show, but I knew that I had just been handed my romantic cards and that suited me. Some things just have to be done for the sake of the nation, but even with people like me there are limits.

'Let's stick to the work, then.'

'That is why I am here. You listen carefully.'

'Very carefully.'

Concisely she laid it all out for me. It was all very neat, and I saw at once that – given goodwill on Bertina's part – then she would be no trouble.

When Suma had finished she stood up and I went to the door with her.

Holding it half open, I said, 'Do you stay here tonight?'

'No. I leave now. But as I said, I shall see you in a few days.'

'And Lian?'

'She has things to do.'

'No business of mine, eh?'

'It is good only to know what you have to know.'

'Well, I know something about Lian. She's got a big thing going for this Arthur Fairlawn.'

Suma smiled. 'Lian is like that sometimes. But it means nothing. While it lasts, it lasts. When it is over then she does not give it one thought. In our work, our lives, how could it be otherwise? You should know that.'

'None better.'

She smiled again and her little hand touched my sleeve. Just for a moment her lips came up and brushed against mine and then she was out of the room. From the doorway

135

I watched her go down the corridor. Hasler was waiting at the door. He opened it for her and they went out together. I heard a key go in the door. I stood there, wondering for a moment or two about Lian. Just how good a character judge was Suma, I asked myself? If it came to that, just how good a character judge was I? I didn't know, but I did know that if you had doubts about anyone then the only thing to do was to take precautions. Just at this moment the voltage in the current trickling up my spine had been stepped up and I knew that I wasn't going to take any chances.

I went into Horace's room for a conference. He didn't give any trouble. Why should he? He didn't believe in taking chances either ... not when he had money in his case and the pleasures of Rome ahead. You work with some people, and you get to like them – and then you have responsibilities. You should always take your responsibilities seriously.

NINE

Wrong Room

I DIDN'T go to bed. People could be as affable and as pleasant as they liked to your face, but in an affair like this there could only be one thought truly uppermost in their minds. Maximum security. They all wanted it. They were all going to try and get it. And maximum security meant silence, complete and permanent. Particularly for small fry.

I put a chair against the wall by the hand-basin, so that when the door opened I should be behind it. I sat there in trousers and shirt sleeves, nursing my automatic. It was a long vigil and the chair was hard so I got a pillow and sat on that. After an hour the chair began to come through the pillow.

He came at one. I didn't hear him until he took hold of the door handle and I heard it turn slowly. He was good. The door opened with less than a sigh of sound. I let him get a few feet into the room, drifting by me like a cloud, and I could suddenly smell his hair pomade.

I switched the light on and stood up.

Hasler was standing by the bed in black shirt, black pants and pink tie. He half turned, surprised, and I saw his right hand holding the nastiest looking knife. There's nothing like a knife for real silent work.

I said, 'Drop the cutlery.'

He turned fully, not dropping the knife, and everything he felt for me was written in Gothic lettering over his face.

'Drop it,' I said. I could feel a nice, warm glow building up inside me, the kind that Miggs always said you must have if you're going to give of your best.

He said, 'This isn't your room.'

Just like that, the cheeky bastard, and I could see that he wasn't worried a bit.

'I thought you might pay a visit to Horace,' I said. 'So we changed rooms. Now – drop the knife before I shoot it out of your dirty hand.'

He didn't drop it. He came for me like a black panther wearing a pink tie.

I was glad about the tie. I knocked his hand up with the automatic, hard, making him let go of the knife which dropped to the floor. With my left hand I grabbed the knot of his tie and jerked him sideways so that he lost his balance. Before he hit the ground I put my knee into his stomach and the wind went from him like a blow out. But it didn't knock the spirit from him.

He came up, faster than I could have thought possible.

It was interesting while it lasted. We were a bit cramped for room which put some of Miggs's more complicated ploys out of court, but even so I think Miggs would have approved of my showing. It took a few minutes to gentle him down and I had to use fist, feet, and twice the butt end of the automatic. But after a little while – and with a certain amount of damage to myself – I had him ready to eat out of my hand if I were prepared for my fingers to be bitten off.

I said, 'Get up, and take me down to him.'

He rolled over on the floor, hugged his diaphragm, and spat at my feet.

I pretended not to have noticed and pulled the door open.

Horace was standing outside.

He said, 'You were right.'

I said, 'Go back to bed. The party's over.'

Hasler stood up and swayed a little.

I said, 'Try walking – and don't stop until we reach Billings or Fairlawn. I don't care a damn which.'

He went past me, head turned towards me and – credit where credit is due – I honestly think he was contemplating

138

having another try. However, he decided not and went into the corridor and I followed.

Horace from my room door said, 'You sure you can handle this?'

I nodded. Privately I wasn't sure of anything except that both Horace and possibly I had been marked as expendable and I was going to have a good try to get our categories changed.

Horace said, 'It's all very upsetting.'

I didn't have any answer to that. I was prodding Hasler in the back with the automatic, to keep him moving towards the wooden door at the end of the corridor.

It was a large conservatory sort of affair. There was a door into it off the hallway just at the foot of the stairs. The door was glass and I could see the two of them over Hasler's shoulder as he pushed the door open.

They were sitting at a small bamboo table which had been pulled up alongside a long water-lily tank sunk into the ground. Down one side, on stands, were six tanks of tropical fish, brightly lit. Billings, I thought, must be a fish-fancier. High up at one end of the place was a little gallery with a run of iron steps reaching up to it. I had a swift impression of a glass roof overhead, glass all around, a wild confusion of creeper stuff all over the place, and big fleshy looking plants in the beds around the walls.

The table was covered with papers and Billings and Fairlawn were doing business over a bottle of Hine's brandy.

Billings looked up as we entered and he frowned. If I had any problems, the frown seemed to say, I could wait until tomorrow. Then he saw Hasler's face, which was no thing of beauty, and his frown deepened.

'What's this, Hasler?' he said.

Hasler just turned and looked briefly at me.

I said, 'Clear out – and keep below stairs.'

Hasler hesitated. Fairlawn leaned back in his chair, hitched the knee of his trousers, and swiftly draped his face in a mantle of casualness. At that moment he must have been doing some hard and fast thinking.

'Do as Carver says,' said Billings.

Hasler went.

'All right, Carver. Let's have it,' said Billings, and he bulked back in his chair and put the tips of his fat fingers together and kept his eyes on me.

I said, 'Your words this morning were that any subsequent breach of security by any member of this household would be a matter of mutual concern and action. Right?'

'That's true.'

'Somebody around here is being too subsequent. I've just had to stop Hasler putting a knife into Horace Goodenough. As a member, ex officio, of the Ta Chung-Hua etcetera etcetera, and so responsible for those working for the People's Republic, I wish first of all to protest and, secondly, to know who gave the order.'

Billings looked down at his finger-tips, rearranged them, and then said softly, 'I find your attitude entirely reasonable.' He then looked at Fairlawn.

I must say, Fairlawn came back without a flicker of hesitation. Looking at Billings and reaching for his brandy glass he said, 'I didn't think you would want to be bothered with it. You've trusted my judgement before and this was only a minor matter. Goodenough has got money and he will find some woman, take a few drinks too many, and then talk. Personally I thought the security risk was better dealt with immediately.'

You'd have thought he was making some statement at a parish meeting about the need to keep the village green clear of litter.

Maybe he was aware of this because he looked at me and reverted to type. 'Sorry, old boy. Can't be too careful. But let's face it, Horace could slip up. However—'

'You can stuff your howevers.' Then to Billings I said, 'You're accepting that?'

He looked from me to Fairlawn and then back to me.

'I disapprove completely,' he said.

'I'm glad to hear it. But your staff relationships seem a bit confused. Why don't you teach your boys the facts of life in this game? You can't use people and then get rid of them. You'd soon run out of helpers.'

'I agree,' he said.

'That makes everything all right,' I said. 'Except at this moment Horace might have been dead.'

Billings said heavily, 'I assure you that you can leave this matter with me.'

'Good,' I said. 'But before I go back to bed I want two points settled.'

'Anything in reason, old man,' said Fairlawn. I saw Billings's face tighten. He didn't like Fairlawn jumping in ahead of him.

'What are they?' Billings asked.

'First – Horace and I leave here together tomorrow morning.'

'Very well,' said Billings. 'And the second?'

'The second,' I said, 'is between Fairlawn and myself.' I turned towards him and I held the automatic on him. Just for a moment, I caught an anxious flicker in his eyes which was pleasant to see, and I said, 'Get this straight, Fairlawn. In Mr Billings's book you may be a big number. You may be worth every penny he pays you for whatever you do. But to me you're just a pain in the arse.'

He looked at me and smiled faintly as I put the automatic in my pocket. His voice creamy with charm, he said, 'Sorry, old boy. Whole thing a ghastly mistake. No hard feelings?'

'None,' I said. I should, of course, have waited for some real cliff edge and made a real job of pushing, but I've got an impulsive nature and I was thinking of Horace and also of Bertina – so I put up my foot to the edge of the chair, which he had tipped back slightly, and I pushed.

He went, literally, base over apex, backwards into the pool and the tidal wave washed around my feet. I turned and walked out. After me, to my surprise, came the sound

141

of Billings laughing. It was a great laugh, a typhoon, the kind that must have convulsed Nero as he watched a handful of crazy Christians being chased around the arena by a hungry lion.

Going back up the stairs, I began to whistle gently to myself. I had that happy feeling that I'd made an enemy for life.

The next morning Horace and I left together. Hasler took us down to the garage. He had a two-inch strip of sticking plaster over his right eye. We didn't exchange any civilities.

The dark blue van was waiting in the garage. Inside, sitting on her travelling case was Bertina. Horace and I climbed in and Hasler locked the door on us. I got a very brief good morning from Bertina.

The drive took over two hours and when we were let out we found ourselves in a big, busy town square. It was drizzling gently.

Leaving the three of us standing under a catalpa tree at the kerb edge, Hasler ducked back into the cab to get out of the rain.

I said, 'Where are we?'

He said, 'Lyon. Down the far end of the square there's a public parking lot. Your car's there. Here.'

He handed me the car keys. He started the motor and then held the gears and looked out at me. I knew what was on his mind.

'Okay,' I said, 'say it and get it off your narrow chest.'

A smile went over his face like an eel slipping down a muddy bank into a stream, and he said, 'Some day, I hope we meet again. God help you then.'

I pulled a long face. 'Now you've really got me worried.'

I turned to Horace who was watching a girl in a plastic mackintosh who was waiting for a bus under the next tree and said, 'You stay here with Bertina. I'll go and get the car.'

Horace nodded without looking at me and said, 'It

142

would make a fine study. Girl under Tree in the Rain.'

I walked off. I didn't think Horace's money would last him long when he got to Italy. He was too susceptible to beauty.

I found the car and drove back to Horace and Bertina. Then I drove to the station, left Bertina sitting in the car with a little thunderhead of a frown on her brow, and went in with Horace.

He got himself a ticket.

'Thanks for everything,' he said. 'And you look after yourself.'

'I'll try.'

He gave me a long look, and then smiled. 'It's all right for me, this kind of thing. I'm a professional. But I've never quite seen you as properly fitting in this kind of life. Take my advice. If you make enough from this job, retire. Take up some relaxing hobby like painting or gardening. Marry a nice little girl and settle down. Domestic bliss and a peaceful mind. Two great jewels.'

'I'll think it over.'

'For about half an hour.'

The train was in and he was watching a woman get into a carriage. She had long legs and a skirt tight over her rump. There was no doubt that it was an engaging sight for a man with money in his case and a long journey ahead of him.

He put out a hand, said, 'God bless . . .' and was gone.

I heard later, much later, that he eventually got as far as Rome where he met a charming Italian widow and married her. She was a real treasure of a woman – who promised to wait faithfully for him until he got out of a two-year stretch in the *Regina Coeli* for some jewellery swindle which he worked on an Italian film star.

Before going back to Bertina I bought myself a Michelin map at the station bookstall, and then put in a *Rouge-sous-rouge* call. I got Casalis after some time.

He said, 'Greetings. Nice weekend?'

I said, 'Did you manage to keep track of me?'

'No. There's been hell to pay about it.'

I said, 'I'm going to a place called Rethel. Hôtel Moderne. You can get in touch with me there. But be careful – I've got the girl, Bertina Brown with me.'

'Lucky you. Let's have the general outline.'

I gave it to him. Then I went out to Bertina.

We drove fifty miles in complete silence. So far as she was concerned I might have been an auto-pilot. In the end, as she showed no signs of thawing out, I decided that I must do something about it. I pulled into a little restaurant place off the road. It had a small garden running down to a river and tables set out on the grass.

'Time for a drink and something to eat,' I said.

She followed me like a sulky schoolgirl and we sat at a table under a willow and were served by a busy French girl who giggled a bit over my French. We had *langouste au gratin* and a bottle of rosé.

I said, 'We're going to be together for a few days. It would be nice to think they might include some conversation.'

She looked at me over her glass and said sharply, 'Why did you get mixed up in this?'

'The money's good.'

'Is that all you think of?'

'Principally.'

'I don't believe it.'

'You mean you're disappointed in me?'

'I think you're a damned fool.'

'You're in it too.'

'I was a damned fool, too.'

'And a bit frightened?'

She didn't answer for a moment. Then she nodded, and said, 'Frankly, yes.'

I said, 'Before we really start slanging one another, perhaps we ought to get some things clear between us. Just what did Billings say would happen to you if you didn't play ball and stay with me for a few days?'

She didn't answer, so I went on, 'I can guess. He'd be

144

very nice about it, of course. But he'd be firm. No London for you until this thing is settled. Otherwise ... well, no girl with your looks wants to have them spoiled.'

She put her glass down, a little clumsily, so that some of the wine spilled.

'I just want to get right away from it all.'

'Of course you do. But you can't – not just yet. Look, I know exactly how you got into this. You met Fairlawn, you liked him for a while, and some time during that period you discovered that he was also Arnold Finch. How?'

'We met his aunt – by accident – on Paddington Station.'

'And he put up some story to you about a business cover, or something equally fishy?'

'No. He told me the truth.'

'And what would happen if you ever opened your mouth?'

'He took me to see Billings. Then I was given the job in the Ascanti.'

'And you've been scared ever since?'

She nodded slowly. 'They were nice about it. But they made it quite clear. And when all the trouble started about the diamond robbery I just had to forget that I'd ever known about Arnold Finch.'

'Do you know what they're going to do with these diamonds?'

'Yes. Billings told me some days ago.'

'He would, the bastard. That was just to put you in deeper.'

'He may be a bastard. But what does that make you? You came into this from your own choice. I don't understand that. I never thought you were a plaster saint – but I hadn't got you marked down as that kind. I was a damned fool – but you went into it with your eyes open.'

I didn't say anything for a moment. Principally because it was one of those awkward moments when you know you have to make a hell of a choice. I wanted to do something

145

for her, but to that I had to have her on my side, trusting me. Even then I couldn't guarantee success. But I had to try.

She sat there, with a little breeze coming off the river ruffling her blonde hair and her blue eyes were very severe. She was scared, but not so scared that she couldn't find room to be angry with me for willingly mixing myself up in this dirty business. It was a compliment to me – and in return I felt that it merited a confidence.

I said, 'You're dead right that I went into it with my eyes open. But – like you – I wasn't given any choice. I may be all sorts of a guy – but there's one thing I'm dead against, and that's drugs. Whether it's drinamyl tablets for teenagers or heroin for the harder cases – I'm against it. And I'm against Billings and company, and against Suma and Lian.'

Her lips gave a tiny curl of disbelief.

'Now you're going to tell me that you're some kind of a policeman.'

'Why do you say that?'

'Because Billings suggested you might be one. I don't think he believed it. But he thought about it – enough to ask me to keep my eyes open during the next few days.'

'Did he?'

'He did.'

'Well, he's dead right.'

She was silent and I reached for the carafe and poured wine into her glass.

I smiled. 'I'm the secret agent type. I'm all for law and order. I'm the guy you read about who walks a knife edge, gets roughed up, kicked around, and triumphs in the end where he falls exhausted into bed with the girl.'

She said, 'What are you trying to do? Play for my sympathy?' She shook her head. 'I know what you are. Money, you want. You latched on to the Arnold Finch thing and then saw a chance of getting a cut.'

'Originally, yes. But then things changed.' I reached out and took one of her hands. It was cold and she let it lie in mine like a dead fish. I said, 'Have you got any way of reaching Billings. Say by phone?'

'I could always call a man named Cadilly in London. He has ways of passing a message.'

'Oh, yes, Cadilly. Well – all you have to do is pass on this conversation. I'd be a dead duck. If not from Billings – then from the people I work for. There's a phone in the restaurant. You can always reverse the charges, even from France.'

She took her hand out of mine.

'Is this on the level?'

'You want the full story?'

'If you've had time to make it up.'

'Okay. But remember this – I'm not working for your sympathy. I'm telling you because I want to help you if I can. Incidentally, there's a warrant out for your arrest in London. Without meaning to, I laid the information which made that possible. Have I got your attention?'

I had.

I gave it to her without let or hindrance, and when I had finished, she said, 'You must be mad.'

'Why?'

'To tell me this.'

'I don't think so. I'm a great judge of character. Anyway, why should you cross me up? I'm trying to help you. Somewhere in this there's got to be a chance to work a bargain with Commander Barnes. And it's got to be a good one to hold him off because he's a bloodthirsty bastard. Do I get your vote of confidence?'

For the first time that day I got a small smile as she nodded her head. She said, 'I'm glad you told me.'

'And you're not going to make a phone call?'

Her hand came out and held mine.

'You know I'm not,' she said.

Later, in the car, I said, 'Tell me – did you get any idea where that house was?'

'No. Only in the country somewhere, and some mountains around.'

'How did you get there?'

'In Dufy's van, like you did.'

'Dufy?'

'He picked me up from the station at Clermont Ferrand. I'd come from Paris. I sat in the back. And then we stopped after about an hour or so. Then when I arrived at the house I saw that it was Hasler driving.'

'Dufy,' I said. 'Who is he? Is he a plump, jolly sort of number with a gold tooth?'

'Yes. He used to be a croupier at the Ascanti, when I first went there. But he retired and came back to France and opened a garage somewhere.'

'He's French?'

'Of course. That's why he came back to France.'

'Where in France?'

'I don't know. At least—'

'Come on, think. Where?'

'I can't remember. I haven't got that sort of brain.'

'But you must have some idea. Think. Dufy. France.'

'Well . . . Oh, wait – we sent each other Christmas cards last year.'

'Then you must have his address.'

'Yes. But I can't remember.'

'Well, you've bloody well got to.'

'And I tell you I can't. If I was in England it would be easy.'

'What do you mean?'

'You're like a terrier, aren't you?'

'I have to be, because it could be important. If I'm going to make a bargain I've got to have something that other people don't know. This could be it. Now – how could you know if you were in England?'

'Because it's in my address book at the flat.'

I had a nice sense of relief. Like the first long pull at a glass of draught bitter on a hot day.

'Just where in your flat is this book?'

'In the top drawer of my bureau. At the back on the left. It's a tan-coloured, diary thing one of the wine suppliers to the Ascanti gave me. His name and address are in it.'

'Good.'

'But we're not in England,' she said.

I reached out an arm and put it round her shoulder.

'We aren't,' I said. 'But other people are.'

Rethel is a little town on the banks of the Aisne, a hundred and ninety-two kilometres from Paris and thirty-eight ditto from Reims. The Hôtel Moderne was opposite the railway station. Two rooms had already been booked for us by Suma.

While we were having dinner I saw, through the glass door of the dining-room, Casalis booking in at the reception desk. He was wearing a false moustache, a beret, and the little rosette of the *Croix de Guerre* in his buttonhole. He looked a dead ringer of a small French manufacturer who had to do his own commercial travelling. He also looked remarkably like Casalis.

Bertina was tired and went up to her room early. At her door she turned and gave me a light kiss on the lips.

I said, 'Sleep well – and don't worry. Things will work out.'

'You think they will?'

'Sure.' I made it sound good.

Her lips brushed mine briefly again.

'A bonus,' I said.

'In a way. You're a good guy and you say things as if you mean them, as if you care about people. Maybe that's why I took to you the first time we met. Christ, I haven't been very bright about all this, have I?'

'We'll fix something. I promise.' I was a great one for making promises without having any clear idea how to carry them out.

She smiled. 'Just like that? You promise. And now I can go to bed and sleep without a care in the world?'

'That's the idea.'

'Boy, you should have sold patent medicine.'

149

I went along to my room, lit a cigarette and sat on the edge of the bed contemplating my toe caps. The only conclusion I came to was that my shoes were dirty. There was a steady tired ache in all my bones which came from sheer nervousness.

The telephone rang and it was Casalis.

He said, 'Baby nicely tucked up with a goodnight kiss and a pat on the bottom?'

I said, 'One of these days you'll unwind and they'll never get the elastic back.'

'There's a car round the corner of the hotel. Peugeot. Red. It's waiting for you.' He rang off.

I went down, still nervous.

Round the corner was the Peugeot and Aristide was at the wheel. I got in beside him.

I said, 'Where? And who?'

He said, 'Sutcliffe and Barnes. Where doesn't matter.'

'Barnes? He's way off his patch, isn't he?'

'No shaking him. He still regards this as his baby.'

'You're telling me. He sees it as his last case before he retires. Barnes bows out in a blaze of glory. Life story sold to the *News of the World* for a packet – and then, maybe, a knighthood.'

We were through the town now and heading out along some country road. I didn't bother to keep track.

After half an hour we ran into a small village and the car stopped in front of the *mairie*. The place was in darkness except for a light in one of the top rooms. Aristide led me in, down a draughty corridor where official notices flapped at us from the wall as we passed. Then up an iron staircase that smelt of disinfectant, and into the lighted room where the first thing I saw was a large photograph of de Gaulle over a fireplace filled with pink frilled paper.

Behind a long table in a leather-backed chair was Sutcliffe. Sitting at the far end of the table was Barnes. I didn't get any cordial greeting. Sutcliffe just pointed a plump finger at a hardwood chair on my side of the table. I sat down, still nervous, and feeling like a candidate for a third-

150

grade clerkship up for interview and without a hope in hell. I looked around the room for help, but there wasn't a sign of a drink anywhere. Why, I wondered, did they always make me feel unwanted?

'Start from the beginning, go slow, and omit nothing,' said Sutcliffe. He wore a dark blue suit, old Etonian tie, and was a real breath of the old country. Barnes was in shooting tweeds with leather patches on the elbows and his face was a great, graven slab like an Easter Island statue.

I cleared my throat which didn't seem as big as usual and started. I gave them everything right up to the time that I had driven away from Lyon station with Bertina. They heard me in silence and when I finished Barnes was the first to speak.

'Just over a million, you say the valuation was?'

'Yes. But it's still quite a big headline, isn't it?'

Sutcliffe got up from his chair, turned his back on me and stared at de Gaulle thoughtfully. At least that's what it looked like from the wrinkles on the back of his neck.

'Let's get this straight,' he said. 'These drugs are coming in by barge down the French canal system?'

'Yes. Suma's going to phone me when and where to meet the barge. She'll be on it when I go aboard, but she's not staying. Bertina and I make the trip. Remembering the cable I saw in her hotel room I shall be surprised if the barge isn't called *La Fauvette* and the master Grognon. E19 foxes me, though.'

Sutcliffe turned.

'E19 is for Ecluse 19. That's Lock 19. Probably where she meets the barge. And I'd say on the Canal des Ardennes – that runs through Rethel.'

Barnes said, 'She said nothing about the hand-over point?'

'No. I'm to know that eventually. All I have to do is stay aboard and keep an eye on things. Suma will join us just before the hand-over. So far as I can see I'm a strongarm man to make sure that the exchange goes without hitch. Both sides have got to trust one another but they're not just leaving it at that.'

Barnes stood up.

'What about this damned girl?'

'What about her?'

'Well, if she's going to be with you and you've got to pass information to Casalis and Aristide she might get wise. In fact, Billings might have planted her on you for just that reason. He wouldn't overlook any possibility.'

'To Billings,' I said, 'she's an embarrassment. So I've got her – until she can return to London.'

'And then I'll have her, by God!' He slapped a big fist into his palm. 'When I think that if she'd given us that Finch-Fairlawn connexion I might have wrapped all this up in England—'

'She's just an ordinary girl who got mixed up. The way you talk she might be the brains behind everything.'

He gave me a sour look. 'Gone soft on her, have you?'

Before I could say anything, Sutcliffe said, 'How do you see the Billings-Fairlawn set-up?'

'So far as I can see they work together all right. Fairlawn overstepped the mark with Horace Goodenough, but that could have been excess of zeal. It's clear what they intend to do. Billings aims to come back to London without a shred of evidence to connect him. He'll pay off his boys there and then live like a king. Fairlawn and Hasler, I guess, are for the wide open spaces and new identities.'

Sutcliffe gave me a long look, and then said gently, 'Go on.'

My nervousness was wearing off a bit now. They weren't being too bad with me. I put on a slightly stupid look and said, 'Go on what?'

Sutcliffe smiled. 'You're not a fool, Carver. It must have occurred to you. Billings wants London and security. Fairlawn wants abroad – and security. They can rely on it from the professionals who worked with them in London. But you and the girl are not professionals. Get me?'

'Yes. I've had similar thoughts. If you really want the truth, I'll settle for out now.'

'You stay,' said Barnes.

I ignored him.

Sutcliffe said, 'You've no idea where this valuation house is?'

'None.'

'Not even the smallest idea?'

'No. Your people had a chance to do better than me. You could have followed. What went wrong?'

Neither of them answered. I lit a cigarette and stared at de Gaulle. I didn't get any sympathy from him. But maybe underneath that heavy Gallic overcast he approved. He knew something, too, about keeping a little in hand.

I said, 'About the girl. As I said – she's a stupid number who really had nothing to do with anything. I'm going to do a hell of a lot for you two. I might even finish up with a knife in my back. It's a risk I'll take happily if I have your promise that all you'll do to the girl is give her a good talking to.'

'She gets what's coming to her.' There was a fine, swelling volcanic rumble in Barnes's voice. 'The bitch.'

'Do you go along with that?' I asked Sutcliffe.

'Why not? The due process of law must be observed.'

'Since when in your service? You don't care a damn for the law if it suits you.'

Sutcliffe smiled and I didn't like it.

'Don't get any chivalrous ideas about her, Carver. I've warned you about that kind of thing.'

'And don't get any other ideas,' said Barnes. 'There's money, big money in this affair. You've got itchy palms. You've already done well. But from now on you're really sitting in the driving seat. I don't want you to get the slightest idea that you can bend anything – for the sake of a blonde-headed floozy with blue eyes or for the sake of a few extra hundred quid. Clear?'

'As mud. And why don't you stop fussing about your tiny blaze of glory? And, as a matter of interest, who is the boss here? You or Sutcliffe?'

Neither of them liked that. Barnes because he knew he wasn't the boss, and Sutcliffe because I'd never used anything but 'sir' or a little cough to name him before. They both gave me cold stares. I stood up and walked to the window. The red Peugeot was waiting outside and I could see the red end of Aristide's cigarette.

Without turning, I said, 'Can I go now?'

From behind me Sutcliffe said, 'Yes. But first I want to make two things clear. One – watch that girl. She may not be as stupid as you think. And she may be in much deeper than you think. And secondly – watch yourself. You're making too strong a plea for her. I don't like that.'

I turned and I wasn't nervous now. I was just plain bloody angry. Neither of them cared a damn for anything except getting this job wrapped up. They'd roped me in, and I was being paid, and they were going to use me without caring a cuss whether I came out the other end walking or carried. Because I was useful just now they had to be reasonably nice to me. But anyone else, like Bertina, who didn't have any use to them, didn't exist as a human being.

I said, 'I didn't care for that kind of talk. I could dig my heels in now and say I won't go an inch farther unless you give me a clearance on the girl. I haven't taken the Queen's shilling, you know. I can just walk out.'

Sutcliffe said easily, 'Try it.'

And Barnes with a mild volcanic grunt said, 'No deal.'

They were right, of course. If I didn't go through with it then anything could happen – to me.

I walked to the door.

'All right,' I said. 'But I'm a soft-hearted type. There's something about a woman in distress that just brings out a rare touch of decency in me. You're lucky not to suffer from it.'

I had my fingers on the door handle when Sutcliffe said, 'Was it something to do with this rare touch of decency which made your conversation with her at lunch so absorbing?'

I swung round, not hiding my surprise.

'So somebody was on our tail from Lyon?'

Sutcliffe nodded. 'One of the Lyon cars. Plain clothes. After you phoned in. They reported a very earnest talk between the two of you. What was the gist of it?'

I smiled. It was an effort and I could feel it cracking a bit at the ends.

'The gist was twofold. One, a discussion on how to make *langouste au gratin* – which no doubt the boys reported we ate. And secondly – since she didn't really want to come with me – a lecture from me on what would happen to her if she went back to London against Billings's wishes. He'd threatened to razor her. Between ourselves we weren't on very good terms.'

'Interesting,' said Sutcliffe. 'Things must have changed, though – since you got two goodnight kisses this evening.'

'Old peeping Tom Casalis, eh? Well – I said we weren't on good terms. But then we had the rest of the day driving and my charm began to tell. Any more?'

They both looked at me; Sutcliffe amused now, and Barnes rubbing his two big hands together as though he was longing for something with life in it to squeeze.

I went out and as the door shut behind me nervousness came down like a mist, cold and thick. If anything went wrong now because of my confidence to Bertina then Wilkins would have to make an announcement in *The Times*. I could see it. Carver, Rex. On the *blank of blank –, suddenly, as a result of being a blank fool*.

TEN

Double Takeover

THE FOLLOWING evening I had a phone call from Suma.
Five minutes later there was another call, from Casalis in
the hotel.

I said, 'That was quick.'

He said, 'We've got the local exchange cooperating.'

I relayed to him the instructions I had been given by
Suma.

At nine o'clock the next morning, Bertina and I checked
out of the hotel. I drove round to the Renault garage which
was in the Rue Gambetta – which was also the main road
out to Reims and to the bridge over the canal. We left the
car and walked down to the bridge, our cases in hand.

A few yards down from the bridge a couple of barges
were tied up alongside. Suma was on the outer one. At a
first glance the barge seemed to be about a hundred yards
long, all battened down hatch covers, with a catwalk
around the sides and, at the far end, a squat wheelhouse
with a command window along its face. A man was lean-
ing against the wheel, smoking. Against the windows of
the lower cabin were neat blue curtains. The door to this
cabin was flanked by two lifebelts which carried the
inscriptions: *La Fauvette – Namur – Entreprise Générale
Grognon Fils*.

Standing in the doorway was Suma, wearing a white
raincoat and a white jockey cap and looking very much
out of place.

Bertina and I went down the footpath from the bridge,
and crossed the deck of the first barge to *La Fauvette*.

Suma gave us a polite welcome. She was in one of her
businesslike moods. She introduced us to Grognon who

grunted something. He was a man of about sixty and although he spoke English he clearly wasn't going to waste it on idle conversation.

Suma took us below. There was a biggish main cabin, the cupboard doors and seat rests all painted with little flowers and animals, and everything was as bright and shining as a P and O engine room. There was a minute galley, a minuter lavatory, and a shower behind a curtain where I would have to bend double, and then three small sleeping cabins.

Suma didn't waste any time.

She said to Bertina, 'Maybe, you like to unpack while I talk to Mr Carver?'

Bertina disappeared into one of the sleeping cabins. Suma sat down on a seat in the main cabin. She fitted a cigarette into the long gold cigarette holder which I had given her as a return present and said, waving it, 'Now I use it always. It was very nice of you.'

I held out her gold lighter and lit the cigarette for her.

I said, 'Is the stuff aboard?'

She nodded. 'Forward in the hold. It is hidden in three cement sacks. All Grognon's cargo is cement for Lyon.'

'Are the Grognon brothers in on it?'

'Only one brother. Yes. He knows. He is very reliable. I joined him yesterday on the Ardennes Canal.'

'Where does the barge come from?'

She smiled. 'You are curious?'

'Naturally.'

'From Antwerp. Down the Albert Canal. Then some of the River Meuse. Then the Canal de l'Est and then down here.'

As she spoke I saw through the cabin window Aristide come down the towing path on a bicycle with a couple of fishing rods tied along the centre bar.

I said, 'And what do I do?'

'All you have to do is to stay aboard a few days. I'll join you later when it is near the time for the exchange. And when we do the exchange you are with me.'

157

'You expect trouble?'

'No. But I always prepare for it.'

'Sensible.'

'I have to be.' She lowered her cigarette and smiled at me. 'Now I go. You have a pleasant time ahead. Once I do this trip some years ago. You just float through France, through the fields and woods. It is a kind of paradise. And you have nice company. You should be very happy.'

'Oh, I am.'

She gave a fuller smile, reached out and touched my hand and said, 'I try not to be jealous.'

I said, 'Billings doesn't know the exchange point yet?'

'Why?'

'I've got to protect the cargo. Pleasure is one thing business is another. If he knew the stuff was coming down in this barge he might try something funny.'

She shook her head. 'Mr Billings is a trustworthy man. Even so, at the moment he does not know how the cargo is coming into the country. When I say it is all right for Bertina to come with you I do not give him any details.'

'Does Lian know?'

'Yes. But her work is finished. She has gone back to London yesterday.'

'Arthur Fairlawn will be heartbroken.'

'Not for long.' She stood up. 'There is more you wish to know?'

'No.'

'Good. Then I see you in a few days.'

I went on deck and watched her go. She walked up to the bridge and headed for the town. I went back below. Bertina was still in her cabin. I took a look in the other two. In one Suma had left her case and some stuff. I took the other and changed into slacks and a sweat shirt. So far as I could see it looked as though it was going to be the kind of cruising I could enjoy; no hauling on bloody wet ropes and getting soaked through, no living, eating and drinking at an angle of forty-five degrees and having to worry about where the wind was coming from before you spat overboard. An even keel and land never more than thirty feet away – that was for me.

When I surfaced, we were under way. Bertina came on deck in jeans and a blue blouse and she looked so good that I had to say a few nasty things under my breath about Barnes and Sutcliffe.

For most of the day we got in Grognon's way trying to help at the various locks. When there was nothing to do we lay on deck in the sun and watched the country go by. The barge had to keep to the canal speed limit of six kilometres an hour. On the open rivers, I learned, you could beat it up to all of fifteen kilometres. We just floated down this narrow highway and there was plenty of time to see what was coming and to have a good look at it while it passed – and that's something that people have forgotten about in modern travel.

That evening we berthed at some small canal village. Grognon came and had a drink with us and then disappeared ashore. He came back late and said he had eaten ashore.

Bertina fried egg and bacon for us in the galley and managed to burn the bacon.

'I'm the world's lousiest cook,' she said.

'Don't worry. From tomorrow I'll take over. A girl with your figure etcetera doesn't have to worry about cooking.'

'She has to worry, though.' Just for a moment a tiny wrinkle creased her forehead.

'No need. I'll get you safely to port.' I meant to, too.

She went to bed before me. I sat in the cabin with a nightcap – Suma had stocked the bar well for us – and thought about the load we were carrying. Up forward somewhere there was enough of the right stuff to complete the ruin of thousands of lives and leave enough over to hook the same number of recruits to keep the business healthy.

In the loo the next morning, I scribbled on a piece of paper: Barge destination Lyon. Cargo aboard. Cargo drop presumably somewhere before Lyon. Route Canal de l'Aisne à la Marne and Canal Latéral to Vitry-le-Fran-çois. Then Canal de la Marne à la Saône, then down Saône. I put this in an empty cigarette packet.

I knew the route because over a drink the night before I had, with hard work, got Grognon to tell me about it.

I went on deck and sat on the upturned dinghy at the stern. Grognon was fiddling about forward somewhere, getting ready to cast off, and Bertina was below over boiling the breakfast eggs. Twenty yards astern of us a bicycle was propped against a willow and Casalis, still wearing his beret, but now in *bleu de travail,* was fishing. Like a confirmed litter bug I jerked the packet into the grass at the canal's edge and then went forward to get in Grognon's way as he got the barge off.

That day was as pleasant as the first and Bertina and I began to get the hang of helping Grognon at the locks. For all his lack of conversation Grognon was a well-known man down the canals. There was a lot of frenzied chit-chat with the other barges we met, hooters blowing and arms waving, as France drifted by. The only things we disturbed were the fishermen or the occasional heron harpooning in the shallows by the banks. It was so peaceful that I could now and then forget about the real job in hand.

Two nights later we berthed in the canal port at a small village called Vouécourt. This was about half-way down the length of the Canal de la Marne à la Saône.

When Grognon came down to have his ritual evening drink with us, he handed me a letter from Suma. The envelope was pretty grubby and I guessed that he had been carrying it ever since she had left. He made no comment, and I read it and made no comment.

After dinner I left Bertina to wash up, which was fair enough since I had done the cooking, and I walked up to the village where there was a small hotel.

I bought myself a glass of porto and some jetons for the telephone. I rang Chambéry 1.18 and asked for Monsieur Billings. He came on almost at once. I wasn't surprised.

The number was probably of some hotel and he had been briefed by Suma to be expecting a call this night. I relayed to him the information which Suma had put in her letter, and then I took my drink out into the small garden that overlooked the river.

Sitting under a brightly coloured Cinzano umbrella and staring at a glass of beer as though it had just said something insulting to him was Casalis. I had seen him walking up to the village just after we had berthed. He'd given up his beret for a panama hat, his moustache was smaller, and he was wearing a shabby brown suit, and he clearly wasn't his usual happy self. He'd done a lot of bicycling in the last few days.

He said, 'This is a bloody lark, this is, following you down this bloody canal, and having to stay at these bloody seedy hotels while you idle along in the lap of luxury and have all the time during the day to make up for the sleep you lose at night.'

'That's right,' I said. 'You staying at this luxury hotel?'

'Yes.'

'Nice. Michelin gives it a knife and fork.'

'Spoon and fork,' he corrected. '*Simple et convenable.*'

'Your agony's nearly over.'

'How come?'

'I've just phoned Billings. Chambéry 1.18 – if that's any help. Probably some handy hotel or restaurant. The dropping place is three days ahead. At a place called Saint-Saveur. That's almost down to the point where the canal joins the river Saône.'

'You're quite the little navigator.'

'I'm learning. Did you know there are a hundred and fourteen locks on the canal and it's two hundred and twenty-four kilometres long with a uniform depth of water of two metres and twenty centimetres, and the headroom under all the bridges is three metres seventy-one centimetres, except at Vitry-le-François which is—'

'Stuff it,' he said. 'Give me the details of the hand-over.'

'It's at the quay in Saint-Saveur. Eight o'clock. A van

161

will call for a small load of cement. Three bags with inner plastic containers. And Suma's coming aboard tomorrow evening. It was all in a letter she left with Grognon for me.'

He rose. 'Well that about wraps it up, doesn't it?'

'For some people, yes. Billings and Co and the Chinese girls. Others don't merit the wrapping.'

'Blondie?'

I nodded. 'I think I could work hard and get Sutcliffe to play. But not that bloodthirsty Barnes.'

Casalis grinned. 'My heart bleeds for you. But you were always a sucker that way. Well, see you at Saint-Saveur. It's a good name, isn't it?' He moved off.

I watched him go. He was like the rest. Do the job and don't muck about with any emotional stuff.

It would have been convenient to be like that. Sometime I promised myself to give it a try. But just now was a bad time. I had to try and promote something for Bertina. All I'd done so far was to have put in a call to Mrs Meld at her home from Rethel asking her to give a message to Wilkins. I wasn't going to speak direct to Wilkins either at her home or the office. Sutcliffe would have those lines monitored still. But was I ever going to have the need to call Mrs Meld again? I couldn't see it. I just couldn't see it. All promise and no show. That was Carver. Saint-Saveur with a broken lance and a spavined mount.

Maybe that was the reason I acted clean out of character when I got back to the barge. Bertina had turned in and, before going into my cabin, I went into hers to say goodnight. She had the small bedside light on and was sitting up, wearing black-and-red striped pyjamas which for comfort or from carelessness she hadn't buttoned fully at the top. She had her blonde hair tied back and she gave me a warm smile as I bent to kiss her goodnight. And that's all I meant it to be, except that the moment my lips touched hers, her arms came round my neck, and arms and lips told me that I was dealing with a woman who had come to a decision. For a while there wasn't much I could do about control. But in the end I did. I sat back and let my breathing settle. She lay back on the pillow giving me a misty blue look and I reached out and slowly did up all the buttons of her pyjama front.

She said, 'What's the matter?'

I said, 'You've got it wrong.'

'Don't you want to?' It was wonderful how big her eyes became with surprise.

'Like hell,' I said. 'Of course, I do. But it comes in the last chapter. After the girl is rescued.'

'Rex . . .' she said. 'To hell with the last chapter.'

I stood up. 'No.'

'What? . . . You really mean that?'

'I think so. If I can get to the door fast enough.'

I took two steps towards it and she came out of her bunk after me and into my arms and her lips were against my lips. She just held on to me for a while and I held on to her.

Then after a time she moved away from me, holding one of my hands, and she said, 'You damned fool . . . You nicest damned fool that ever was . . .'

I kissed her hand, and said, 'Get back into bed before I stop being a damned fool.'

The next day we did about fifty kilometres, down to a place called Rolamport, and berthed just below the road bridge that crossed the canal. The following night we were due at a place called Courchamp, and the night after that at Saint-Saveur. In all we had about a hundred and thirty odd kilometres to do and Grognon was spacing out his daily runs to get us there for the evening of the third day.

Suma came aboard about seven and took up residence. Her letter had said she would.

She was in one of her light-hearted moods and there was a lot of laughter as we all three had drinks before dinner. Seeing her there, wearing one of her exotic Chinese gowns, my gold holder cocked elegantly in one hand, it was hard to imagine that she wasn't just enjoying a pleasure trip.

Round about ten Bertina went to bed and I went ashore

to stretch my legs, leaving Suma in the cabin. I made a
ritual of a stroll along the bank each evening, not just for
exercise, but to give Aristide or Casalis a chance to contact me if they wanted to do so.

I went about a hundred yards up the bank where the
canal curved away, putting me out of sight of the barge,
and there I found Aristide. He was sitting back under a
willow smoking, smacking his neck now and again
against the mosquitoes which had started their evening
foray.

I sat down beside him and said, 'Make it quick. Suma's
aboard – and, anyway, I don't want to be bitten to
death.'

Aristide said, 'All you have to do at Saint-Saveur is to
stay aboard and keep Suma covered. We'll pick the others
up on the quay.'

I said, 'I have a feeling that Billings may not be there.
He's not the kind to show himself in the open if he can
avoid it. That's Fairlawn's job.'

'Once we have the others, we'll find him.'

I said, 'It's a pity the girl Bertina is being dragged into
this. She adds up to less than nothing, and—'

'My friend,' said Aristide, 'don't try that one on me. She
was a fool – and that's an offence.'

'Like hell it is.'

He smiled. 'You can do nothing for her. Forget her.'

Good advice. But, as usual, it didn't help much. I was in
a pretty mixed-up mood as I went back aboard. Suma had
gone to bed, so I had a large whiskey as nightcap, a specific
for more ills than most people will admit, and finally went
into my sleeping cabin.

I was up with the lark the next morning and out in the
galley to make morning coffee for the girls. Through the
little window I could see a field of mustard across the canal
in full flower, a golden yellow that hurt the eyes. There was
a mist coming up off the water in tiny, floating scarves
of pure gossamer. Up on deck old Grognon was whistling
to himself as he polished brass-work. A boy went cycling

164

down the canal path with a basket of long loaves on the carrier.

Life should have been wonderful. But I had only a handful of hours left in which to find some way of saving Bertina from Barnes. And I didn't have a clue.

It wasn't easy taking her coffee in and kissing her good morning.

When I took in Suma's coffee, she rolled over and slowly sat up in bed. She rubbed her eyes and bade me good morning. I set her coffee down beside her and sat on the end of the bunk. She smiled at me as she sipped at her coffee. Then she put it down, reached for her handbag, and took out her cigarettes and holder. I held my lighter flame out to her. She leaned back against the pillows, smiled at me again, and then blew three tiny smoke rings. They broke and frittered away in front of my eyes.

But I wasn't bothering about smoke rings. My eyes were on the cigarette holder. The woman facing me was using a long ivory cigarette holder instead of the gold one which I had given her. Just for a moment, like a fool, I was about to remark on it.

We did talk for a bit, and then I stood up, nodding at her coffee cup, 'More?' I asked.

She shook her head and said, 'No thank you. Now I just enjoy my cigarette.'

I went up to the head of the bunk to get her cup. Standing there I ran one finger down the side of her neck and then I let my hand slide caressing over the naked brown shoulder, down the length of her left arm and so took her hand and raised it to my lips.

'This morning,' she said, 'you are very gallant.'

'This morning,' I lied, making it sound good, 'I wish it was just not simply business between us.'

But all the time I was thinking of a slipping knife and a cut thumb; and a small scar which must still be there if this were Suma and not Lian.

'For us,' she said, 'we have had our pleasures. Always now is business.' She gave a little laugh. 'Besides – if

165

Bertina sees you – you make her jealous.'

For a moment her hand was close to my eyes. No mark on the thumb. No Suma. This was Lian.

I went on deck and Grognon called some greeting as he sluiced a bucket of water down the catwalk. I went ashore and walked up the canal.

The girl in the cabin was Lian – and clearly the switch had been made while I was having my chat with Aristide and Bertina had retired to her cabin. What were the two girls playing at? Whatever it was, they had slipped up over the cigarette holders. Anyway, what was the purpose of doing a switch and clearly intending to keep it from me? I didn't like that, and I began to feel angry. I went back aboard and sat down at the main cabin table. As soon as Lian came out I was going to tackle her. A few seconds later I was glad that I hadn't gone into Lian demanding an explanation. A yard from me, almost hidden in the gap between a seat and a back cushion of the bench on which I sat, I saw a thin gleam of gold. I reached out for it. It was Suma's gold holder.

It was then that I felt really worried. When I'd gone out to see Aristide, I'd left Suma sitting at the table smoking. The holder I'd found was a good two yards from where she had been. Cigarette holders won't roll that far unless there is something to knock them pretty violently from a hand or a mouth.

Violently, that was the word. And it brought a lot of fresh ideas into my mind. I went on deck to sort them out and found myself helping Grognon to cast off and get going.

Only one thing was clear to me. If Lian had given herself away to me, I didn't mean to give myself away to her. And if I wanted to get any kind of truth, it was clear that I had to play this day through just the same as any other day on the barge. The one thing I wanted to do now was impossible until the evening.

It was a long day, and one of the longest performances

166

I had ever given of a man with nothing in particular on his mind.

That evening – the next day we were due at Saint-Saveur – we pulled into the barge port at Courchamp. There was no other barge there. A small dirt road ran down from the side of the bridge to the off-loading quay. The village was two or three hundred yards away. After we had tied up the usual routine took place. Grognon wandered off to the village to get himself a drink and to buy some cigarettes, and have a chat with old acquaintances.

I went into the main cabin. I had slipped a torch and my automatic into my pocket. Both the girls were in the cabin and we sat having a drink and chatting. I knew then what it was to itch with impatience.

Finally, I said I was going on deck for a breath of fresh air before dinner.

Apart from the long run of deck hatch covers which had to be removed for unloading, there were two entrances to the hold. There was a small hatch immediately below Grognon's wheel room, and another right up forward. It was just getting dark and a few bats were out, cutting the air into jigsaw patterns, and the odd cottage light was beginning to show through the trees from the village.

I drew the bolt on the flap of the forward hatch, lifted it, had a quick look around in case Grognon might be on his way back, and then slipped through it and dropped the flap above me.

I switched the torch on and began to make my way aft. There was no headroom and I had to crouch all the way along the small path that had been left between the stacked bags of cement.

I reached the after end. A space was clear of cement, against the bulkheads. A loose pile of tarpaulins had been dumped there. I flashed the torch around. For a moment I felt a sense of relief – then, from under the top tarpaulin I saw a foot protruding. I pulled away the loose canvas. Suma was lying there, on her side, and one arm was thrown up and her cheek rested on it. She was naked except for a pair of brief pants. There was a gag around her mouth and, if for nothing else, I was glad of that for it wiped from my mind any fleeting thought that Bertina could be involved in this. Suma had been silenced quickly to stop Bertina hearing anything in her sleeping quarters.

As the torch light held her, I could have thought that she was sleeping, except that her eyes were wide open, the torchlight reflected dully in them. There was a knife deep in her back.

ELEVEN

One Damned Thing after Another

I WENT down into the main cabin. Lian had changed into a Chinese gown. It had a tight little black collar at the neck, and a green background with a great spray of cherry blossom running across her breasts. She was sitting on the corner of the cabin table, legs crossed, showing a lot of thigh through the slit at the side of the gown, in her hand she was holding what I knew would be a glass of champagne and vodka.

She looked up at me and the cabin lights ran across her dark hair. She said, 'Ready for another drink?'

I nodded and she smiled. It ought to have been Suma, and it wasn't. She put a cigarette in her ivory holder and waited for me to come round and light it. I did. And I was thinking hard.

I said, 'Where's Bertina?'

She said, 'She was tired and said she'd have a little sleep before dinner.'

'Tired?'

She nodded.

I went through to the cabins. I wasn't now in a mood to take her word for anything. I opened Bertina's door and looked in. She was lying on the bed, her back to me and snoring very gently. It was a pretty snore. It had to be. She was a pretty girl.

I went back to the main cabin and made myself a whiskey and water.

Lian said, 'You are very fond of her?'

'She's a nice girl,' I said. 'Pity she ever got mixed up in all this.'

She smiled. 'You like her very much. I can tell. But she

is not really your kind. She is too soft. Not clever enough. When you marry it must be someone very special.' She slid off the table and sat down.

'When I collect my money from this deal,' I said, 'I'm thinking of advertising. Exceptional woman wanted for a very ordinary man.'

She giggled, and it could have been Suma. Only Suma was dead in the hold, a knife in her back. And no matter what Suma had been, no matter how much drug-traffic was a filthy business, dead was dead.

I sat down on the bunk seat and I pulled the automatic from my pocket and put it on the edge of the table, close to me and well away from her.

She looked at the automatic and then at me, and there was no change on her face. The inscrutable oriental. Watch yourself, Carver, I told myself, because she will have more tricks than a circus full of Chinese conjurers.

'So she was tired,' I said.

'Bertina?'

'Yes.'

'Oh, yes. Very.'

'What did you give her?' I asked. 'A quick shot with a hypo, or a glass of drugged gin?'

Her face showed nothing for a moment and then the tiniest hint of a smile flickered about her mouth.

'Lemonade,' she said. 'When you went out. You were very quick to notice.'

'I've heard drugged people snore before. When did you plan to fix me up?'

She gave another of her little giggles and it wasn't nice to hear.

'When you had your second drink. I was going to make it for you.'

I was committed now. If I didn't come out on the credit side I knew that Sutcliffe would kill me for it. I'd let myself get emotional and acted on it. That was right against the book. But the book could go to hell.

I said, 'You're a first-class oriental bitch.'

Her face hardened at that. No smile. Her eyes narrowed a little.

'I do not like those words,' she said.

'I didn't mean you to. I've been down in the hold.'

Calmly she said, 'I knew you had. There's cement dust on your back. How did you guess?'

'You missed one trick,' I said. I took the gold cigarette holder from my pocket and slid it across to her. She picked it up and gave it the briefest of glances, her fingers rolling it absently to and fro. 'I bought this holder for Suma. Since then she's always used it.'

She was completely with it now, knowing exactly where she stood, no doubt thinking fast, wondering what line to take.

She shrugged her shoulders and jerked the holder back hard at me. I made no attempt to retrieve it because I could see her eyes on the automatic. The holder slid off the table to the floor.

I said, 'She was your sister. And you got rid of her just like that.' It didn't sound like my voice. It was coming up from fathoms deep, from some cold, arctic chasm.

'I hated her.'

I nodded. 'I think she guessed it, too. That's why she had me aboard. She felt you might pull something. What is it? You and the Billings crowd? You all walk off now with diamonds and drugs? Nice haul. But you had to kill her first.'

'Yes, I killed her!' Her voice rose suddenly in pitch. 'She was so damned clever, so right. Suma with the brains. Suma always the one with the secret instructions.'

'Who put you up to it? Fairlawn? Did he sell it to you and then to Billings? Sounds like his idea of a good business deal. The bastard.'

'No. It is my idea. Mine. Now, for the first time in my life, I fall in love with someone. I want to live like an ordinary human being—'

'So you start by killing your sister. You think your government will ever let you get away with this?'

171

'To hell with my government! Long ago, when I am a young girl, they cheat me. They make me what I am. Now I cheat them. Now I go away and have a real life with the man I love.'

'So Suma had to die.'

She gave a thin laugh. 'Suma. Always everyone think of Suma. She was a devil, I tell you. You think she liked you? You think you do something special to her? You are a fool. You, she was using too. Why you think at Divonne she make me arrange that business on the golf course?'

I put my hand on the automatic. I wasn't trusting her an inch. She could talk fast – and she could act fast. The talk might be lies. But any action would be dead earnest truth.

'You arranged the golf thing,' I said.

She shook her head.

'Suma make me arrange it because she wanted a final check on you. "Put him in danger," she said, "and then if some other side is guarding him, they will do something to save him." And somebody did. But you were clever about it – so she could not be absolutely sure. But she is always careful. Since then she consider always that you might be working for the police.'

'Good try,' I said. 'So Suma thought I might want to spoil this exchange – and she keeps me working with her all along. What for? So that I'll have the information about the exchange taking place at Saint-Saveur to pass on to my people?'

She was easy now. I could see it and I didn't like it. And no matter what I told myself, there was an edge of doubt in my mind.

She said, 'Whatever Suma was, she was no fool. Oh, no – she was so clever that sometimes I could have killed her before this. But always her cleverness works – until this time when it is I who want something to be different. You think it was difficult for me to arrange things with Grognon? For money, he does anything – that is his life. You know what Suma says about you?'

'Make it good,' I said. 'I've been having bad character references lately.'

'Suma admits it is possible that you work for the police. To her that is no problem. We have met this before. So we bring you in to work for us. It is safer that way. But if you tell your people that it is Saint-Saveur where the exchange takes place – that is what we want you to tell them. We use you. Suma arrange it. But, in fact, the exchange takes place here at Courchamp. At this place, here, tonight. You look surprised.' She laughed. 'Suma herself say that you are not so clever to think of anything like that yourself. You are a nice man, doing too difficult a job for your brains – so you are easy to handle. All this Suma say about you and we have good laugh over—'

'Shut up,' I said brutally.

She shrugged her shoulders. 'You say shut up and I shut up. But one thing first. You should be glad Suma is dead. What I do for her, she planned for you this very night – once you had helped her to see the exchange goes right.'

I didn't say anything. Every word she said might be true. Suma was no fool. I hadn't thought of the Saint-Saveur trick. She was dead right. The job was too difficult for my brains. If I wanted to get out of it everything would have to be fast. But, no matter how fast I acted or thought, one thing was certain, this neat scooping into the net of diamonds, drugs and the people involved, which Sutcliffe was relying on, would never come off. All I could do was to save something from the mess – and the only thing I could save was the cargo stored in the hold. At any moment now a lorry might come down the dirt track to the quay with Billings's boys. If I kept the drugs from them it would be the one good mark amongst the dozen black ones I'd run up against my name.

I stood up slowly, watching her all the time, and I held the automatic on her.

'Okay,' I said, 'maybe I'm all you've said, doubled. But one thing is for sure. You're not taking off with Fairlawn

173

to some luxurious hide-out. Now – just turn round and walk into the sleeping cabin. There's a good lock on the door and you're staying there while I go for Grognon and make him cast off.'

She didn't argue. She just turned and began to walk out of the cabin, through the little galley space, past the shower niche and offices, and into her sleeping cabin and I walked behind her. From the doorway I saw her right into the cabin where she stopped and turned to me. She was smiling, and it was a big, friendly smile, the kind I had seen a hundred times on Suma's face, and she said, 'You are very stupid.'

And then it happened. He came out of the shower compartment. I caught the sound of the plastic curtain swinging, so that I had time to turn just enough to see Hasler's face as he smashed me across the side of the neck.

I went over sideways, my automatic flying from my hand, and I landed with my head and shoulders lying partly in the main cabin.

I opened my eyes from the shock of falling and the first thing I saw was Fairlawn come down the cabin steps fast and over to me, a big smile on his face as though I were the one man in all the world he wanted to meet.

I twisted and started to get up and Hasler slammed me again from behind. I collapsed at Fairlawn's feet.

'Tough titty, old man,' he said. 'Nice to see you putting up such a good show. A complete bloody waste of time, of course.'

It was habit not commonsense that made me try again. But I didn't get farther than my knees. Hasler, who couldn't have been putting out full power before, slammed home an ace and I went out into darkness.

Somebody had his hand over my mouth and was making it difficult for me to breathe. I shook my head but the hand still stayed clamped to me. There was a noise, too, like the sound of some gigantic bath running out, gurgling and swishing.

174

I opened my eyes. Somewhere behind me was a faint light. My head swam and I had to close my eyes, but as I did so I realized that it was not a hand clamped across my mouth. I had been gagged, and my ankles bound. My wrists were tied together behind my back.

The giddiness went from my head and I opened my eyes again. This time they stayed open, and this time I got the whole picture, not too well illuminated, but clear enough to jerk me sharply back to reality.

I was in the hold of *La Fauvette*. The light came from a small, naked bulb. I was about twenty feet from the after end in a small gap between the piled cement sacks. Lapping at the upper edges of the sacks on which I rested was water. It was moving, scummed with a dry film of loose cement that moved and twisted away in crazy arabesques.

I got it then. I was sitting here with the cocks of the hold opened and the barge fast filling with water. Outside it was dark and *La Fauvette* was settling quietly into the deep water at the quayside. She was full loaded, with no more than a foot of freeboard. In the darkness she would settle quietly, no one noticing – and that would be that. It would be a couple of days before anyone could raise her and find what was left of me.

I struggled to a sitting position and one of the sacks under me slipped. I rolled off into the water and went under up to my thighs. There was a good two feet of water in her already.

I hoisted myself back out of the water, but by now it was already lapping over my sacks. As I did so, I saw Bertina.

She was lying on her side, a couple of yards from me, on a pile of sacks a little higher than mine. She was bound and gagged, too, her wrists tied behind her like mine.

Her eyes were open and she was watching me. Just a pair of eyes watching me, frightened eyes.

Anger came into my throat. They'd got it all nicely worked out. Two birds with one stone. When the money is big enough, you've got to protect yourself. Don't be

175

embarrassed by uncertain elements. Just get rid of them. And that was what was going to happen in an hour from now . . . unless Carver did something.

I rolled closer to Bertina and she struggled to a sitting position. We looked at one another, a couple of mutes, and I gave her a nod which was meant to be reassuring. No need to worry. Carver had it in hand. But the trouble was that Carver had nothing in hand.

I edged close to her. She let her shoulders fall against me and I could feel the involuntary shake of her body. Her face, close to me, was streaked with wet cement marks, her hair was loose, and the water in the hold was already lapping around her skirt.

Come on, Carver, I said to myself. Come on. There's got to be something. There had to be something – unless we were just going to sit here, while *La Fauvette* quietly went under.

At that moment, the barge lurched a little as it settled, and a few yards away some sacks slid from their pile and splashed into the rising water. At that moment, too, something lurched in my mind.

Would they, I thought? Would they have been so bloody efficient? But even as I was thinking it I was easing myself off the sacks, away from Bertina.

I dropped into the water, away from the sacks, in the clear runway along the side of the cargo. The water came well above my chest now. I looked back, saw Bertina's eyes on me, gave her a nod, and then I began to work my way on my bottom, legs in front of me, towards the after end of the hold.

As I moved towards the place where I had last seen Suma, I came under the light and could see more clearly. Working through the water, like some clumsy crab, slipping sideways at times because the cement dust on the boards had turned to mud beneath me, I prayed that Fairlawn had made one mistake.

I reached the after end of the hold and looked for the pile of tarpaulins on which Suma had been placed. The water was high up the side of the last pile of cement sacks. I scrabbled round it.

The light was almost dead overhead. Rising out of the water I could just see the wet run of a shoulder and a bare leg and thigh.

I didn't like what I was going to do, but I had to do it. I turned round and backed up to the body, groping behind me for it with the free fingers of my bound hands. I felt her neck, a loose tangle of hair, and I leaned over to one side a bit and fumbled my hands down her back.

I touched it, hard and firm under my fingers, and for a moment I couldn't do any more. Then I got my free fingers cupped tight around it. I let myself go forward.

The knife came out of her back more easily than I had imagined it would. I went forward, face first into the water, rolled and coughed as I swallowed, and then I was sitting up. That was when despair really took over. In the unexpected pitch forward I had dropped the knife!

It took me God knows how long to find it. I pivoted round, feeling with my feet, sliding and stabbing at the slippery cement flooring. Twice I thought I'd got it and was disappointed. Then I felt it and had to go full under water, back first, groping with my hands to get it. I came up and sat, coughing and wheezing like an old man, for a few minutes before I could get moving.

It seemed to take ages to get back to Bertina, to work myself up to her, holding the knife behind me, knowing that our lives depended on it.

I got up to her and half turned to her, nodding over my shoulder towards my hands behind me, which were just above water. For a moment or two she didn't get it. I made angry, impatient noises through my gag. Then she saw the knife. I made a motion with my head for her to turn round, to get her back to me. I couldn't risk trying to let her take the knife. One slip and it would have been away into the dark waters that were rising round us. She turned and, like a blind man, I held the knife, leaving a few fingers free so that I could position the tight nylon cord they had used.

I got the knife up above her wrists so I could work down against the cords towards her hands. I forced myself to work gently, feeling each cord go after what seemed an infinity of slow, sawing movement. As I worked I could sense the straining in her arms and hands as she helped me.

Suddenly there was no resistance to the knife. Her hands were free. She turned and I felt the knife taken from me. . . .

The water was well over the top of the sacks as we slid off them to the runwalk down the side of the hold. I held her hand, leading the way, and there was so little head-room that we had to crouch and the water was up to our necks. Working our way aft I realized that it had risen far more quickly than I had imagined it would because of the bulk of the cement bags.

At the after end the light was still burning, less than a foot above the black water which was alive with little golden snakes of ripples from its reflection. I didn't look to the right where Suma lay hidden, but as I pushed up the hatch cover, I gave her a silent thank you and goodbye. It was the only genuine moment of deep, sincere emotion that had ever passed between us – and I felt dirty and cheap. But grateful. I had to be. It was better to be alive and disliking myself than to be dead.

From the deck Bertina jumped ashore to wait for me while I went down to the cabins to try and collect some of our things. Water was high in our cabins and none of the lights worked now. I groped around, knowing what I wanted and finding most of the things. But the barge gave another sudden lurch and I knew it was going so I made for the deck.

As I jumped ashore the barge went. There was a sudden weird whistle of sound as the last of the air was forced up out of the long hold, and then the bulk of her went slowly under, settling with dignity to leave just the high rise of the after-works above water.

I turned from looking at it and a shape moved quickly

178

up from the darkness. Just for a moment I thought it must be Bertina.

Then a familiar man's voice said, 'What the hell goes on here?'

It was Casalis.

I said, 'Whatever it is – you would have been a bit too bloody late to do much good!' And hearing my own words I realized for the first time that I was shaking with anger.

He said, 'You didn't show up tonight so—'

'Forget it!'

I dropped the stuff I was holding in my arms and then jerked my right hand out at him. I got his wrist and twisted him round, bringing him back hard up against my chest.

'Carver, for Christ's sake—'

'Quiet.'

He was quiet and he didn't struggle. He knew better than that. I had him in a Miggs's hold which needed very little more to tear his arm from his shoulder socket. I slipped my free hand to his right pocket and slapped it.

He said, 'Holster under my left arm. Though God knows why I should help a fool like you. Just—'

'I'll do the talking.'

I reached round and got his gun. Then I increased the pressure on his arm a little and he began to walk. He had to if he wanted to stay whole. I took him across the quay towards a pile of rough timber planks I had seen there earlier and the curious thing was that, although I was still blazing with anger, a nice, warming, comforting anger that had nothing to do with him, there was also a fine sort of singing happiness in my head because I'd just seen it, just seen the edge of a way out.

Only when I had him jammed up against the face of the planks did I feel a little bit sorry for him. It was just his bad luck that he'd caught me at the peak of a discovery. Given time, he would forgive me one day.

Hard against the planks, he said, 'I hope you know what you're doing?'

'I've a rough idea. And don't think there's anything personal in this.'

I raised his gun and hit him. He went down and I bent over him. He had some money and I took it. And he had a torch and I took that. Then I rolled him over and took his jacket and trousers. They would be a bit big for me but they were dry. He made funny breathing noises as I did all this. When he came to, he was going to be in an unforgiving mood. . . .

I went back, collected the rest of the things from the canal side where I had dropped them and, as I stood up laden, Bertina joined me from the shadows.

She didn't say anything. She took my arm and we moved away fast down the canal path, away from the bridge and the village from which a few lights showed. She came with me, silent, and I didn't try to break the silence because I knew that she was walking in the tag end of a nightmare and that, too, only time cures.

TWELVE

Qui est Bloody Well Là?

TWO MILES down the canal, I turned off a side track through a small wood. Beyond it, at the edge of a field, we found a small barn and went inside. There were a couple of bales of straw in one corner. I dropped the bundle I had been carrying, and broke the straw bales up to make a big bed. Somewhere in the rafters overhead a couple of hens made a cackle of protest.

As I finished, Bertina came to me. I put my arms around her and held her tight. It was good medicine for shock.

When I released her, she said, 'What do we do?'

I snapped on the torch, and nodded to the bundle.

'I grabbed some of Suma's things. Get changed.'

'But what are we going to do?'

'Get dry – then have a sleep till first light.'

I began to strip off my wet trousers and shirt. I'd brought for myself from the cabin only my wallet with money.

I said, 'Give me your things.'

I took our wet clothes, went to the barn door and wrung them out. There was a hurdle just inside the door and I spread them on that. I was doing all these things mechanically, and I was thinking hard. I had to because from this moment on we were both in the soup. Both of us abandoned. She more than me. And that was the thing that worried me. Sutcliffe was far too intelligent to think that I would have tried such a double-cross as giving him a false transfer point for diamonds and drugs. But Barnes would. He would believe anything. But no matter how understanding Sutcliffe might be, he would never, once he got his hands on me, let me loose again in France. From his point of view my usefulness was finished – and a damned mess I'd made of things for him. But I just had to be loose in France.

I went back and lay down in the straw alongside her. She reached out and took my hand.

She said, 'I don't think I'm going to sleep yet.'

'All right – let's talk. But keep it low.'

Quietly, she said, 'How could he do it? How could a man you think you know, be such a stranger?'

'Men like Fairlawn,' I said, 'are strangers even to themselves. Now you listen to me, because I've got a lot to tell you. So far as I'm concerned, I can talk my way out of any trouble coming to me. I was played for a sucker. But with you – it's different. You really are in trouble. And there's only one way out.'

'I can't see any.'

'I can. Billings and Fairlawn are away with diamonds and drugs. Sutcliffe will go after them, but he doesn't know any more than I know. What we've got to do – is to get to them before him. We've got to get our hands on the diamonds – because that's the prize Barnes wants. We've got to get them and hold them somehow so that I can do a trade. They get the diamonds in return for giving you a clean sheet.'

'It's impossible.'

'Sure. But I'm going to try.'

She said, 'I've really messed things up for you, haven't I?'

I said, 'Not all that much. Even if you weren't involved I'd want to get my hands on those drugs. It's the one business that really gets me hot under the collar. It's a dirty racket. If I can stop it and also help you at the same time – then so much the better.'

She put out a hand and touched my cheek. 'Even if you can't do anything for me, I'll always know that you wanted to. That'll be a nice thing, at least, to cheer me in Holloway.'

I said, 'Go to sleep.'

She said, 'I can't.'

182

I said, 'Count sheep.'

She said, and I knew hope was beginning to make a spurt, 'Cement sacks would be easier. Where did you get the knife?'

'From a friend.' I hadn't told her about Suma, and didn't intend to.

'You said that in a funny way.'

'It was a funny kind of friendship.'

The next morning, at first light, beyond the wood we found a small country road and a labourer's bicycle propped in the ditch. I could see him hoeing between young sugar beet in the middle of the field that flanked the wood. I pinched his bicycle, put Bertina on the cross bar, and rode a few kilometres to a small village called Champ-litte-le-Prélot. I abandoned the bicycle outside the village. Then, since we had dried off to something approaching a respectable appearance, we walked into the place. There was a parking lot in the main square and it was filling up for the morning market. We loafed around the place for ten minutes and finally swiped a Peugeot saloon. We headed south down the N67 to a town called Gray about 20 kilometres away. In the car dash pocket there was a packet of Gitanes tipped cigarettes – which I welcomed – a Michelin pocket map of the French *Grandes Routes,* and a baby's feeding bottle full of milk which made Bertina feel guilty. Just outside Gray, we turned down a side road and left the car. Then we walked into the town, keeping an eye open for road checks. We sat in a small café and had a coffee while I studied the map. The main thing I knew was not to leave any indication of the way we were heading.

From the café, I put in a call – reversing the charges – to Mrs Meld in London and gave her a simple message for Wilkins.

My wallet with my money was in my jacket. I had an automatic and Casalis's coat and trousers, and I was willing to travel. I bought a cheap suitcase, in case we had to stay in an hotel.

183

The next move was to the railway station, but I checked that carefully before I used it. I bought tickets for Lyon, with a connexion to be made at Dijon.

By two we were in the train. We hit Dijon just before six and, since we had plenty of time to spare, we had a leisurely meal in the station buffet. Then I went along to the ticket office and – although I had through tickets to Lyon from Gray – I bought two tickets from Dijon to Paris and asked for them in English so that I might be remembered.

Then I rang up Mrs Meld again. It wasn't the first time Wilkins and I had used her when we knew that the office phone, my flat phone and Wilkins's home phone would all be monitored.

Mrs Meld said, ' 'Ullo, there, Mr Carver. You 'aving a nice time?'

'Couldn't be better,' I said.

'They've been and fixed your coffee grinder.'

'Fine.'

'And Meld himself put a new washer in the lavatory cistern.'

I said, 'Fine. Is she there?'

'Right here,' said Mrs Meld.

Wilkins came on.

'You're in a mess again, I suppose?' she said.

'Mildly,' I said. She was cross and I knew that it was just pure, warm-hearted anxiety for me.

'They – ' she said, 'have been swarming all over the office and questioning me. One followed me to your flat. He thinks I'm in there still.'

I smiled to myself at the thought of Wilkins dropping out of my bathroom window and slipping into the Meld house. This was pure devotion.

'You're a great girl,' I said, 'and I'll see that you get that electric typewriter the moment I'm back.'

'If you ever do.'

'Stop casting horrorscopes,' I said, 'and tell me what I want to know.'

'It was there all right,' she said grudgingly, and she gave me the information.

'That's fine,' I said. 'You've made my day.'

'Are you sure that you know what you're doing, because—'

'Don't fuss,' I said. 'And don't bother to climb back into the flat. Slip round the corner by the Meld back entrance and let him cool his heels. Bye.'

Bertina and I hung around until about twenty minutes before our train was due to leave before I put in a call to police headquarters in the town – *Rouge-sous-rouge* – and asked for Aristide. I was through to him within two minutes.

I said, 'You know who this is, of course?'

He said, 'Yes.'

I said, 'Is there anyone in the room with you?'

'No.' He sounded very guarded.

'Good,' I said. 'If you want it that way – you can keep this to yourself, but I don't mind.'

'I keep nothing to myself, Monsieur Carver.' Guarded and formal.

'Just as you wish. First – I had nothing to do with bitching up the exchange. They planted a wrong day and place on me.'

'Possibly.'

'Definitely. And for reasons which are highly personal I have to follow a line of inquiry entirely on my own. But I want to ask two favours.'

'Monsieur, you are not in a position even to ask one.'

'With you I am – because if you don't think I'm on the level, no one will.'

'It is debatable.'

'First – will you keep the *Rouge-sous-rouge* system open for me?'

He hesitated, and then said, 'Yes, it can do no harm.'

'Secondly – you know what happened to *La Fauvette*?'

'Yes.'

185

'Has there been any Press release?'

'Not yet.'

'Can you fix one?'

'If I wish.'

'Aristide,' I said, 'basically, I'm on your side. Fix it. I want to see a Press announcement that three bodies were recovered from the barge. Two female, one male.'

'You ask a lot.'

'I might be able to give a lot.'

'We've had a frogman down – there is only one body.'

'But will you fix it that there were three bodies for the Press?'

'Monsieur Carver, I should urge you—'

'Don't. I've got my own urges.'

'I hope for your sake that they are valid.'

'They are. I hate the drug traffic as much as you. I've made myself a promise that Billings isn't going to have those drugs. So just fix the Press release.'

'Well . . .' There was doubt in his voice.

I rang off. And I knew that whatever small percentage of trust he had in me, he would now be moving to trace the call.

Ten minutes later, Bertina and I were in a carriage by ourselves on a slow train to Lyon. She rested her head back against the cushions and smiled at me, her pale hair untidy, her blue eyes shining.

'The thing about you I like,' she said, 'is that you make people feel so good. I'm beginning not to worry.'

'The thing about you,' I said, 'is that you're a susceptible idiot. You don't look where you are putting your tiny feet down. You expect things to be as you want them to be. They aren't – they're always much worse. I know – I make a living from it. A girl with any sense would have seen through Arthur Fairlawn at once. Grow up.'

'Yes, darling. Did you get Dufy's address?'

'Wilkins did. He's got a garage, just outside Grenoble . . . We're going to have a chat with him.'

The next morning – after I had found a barber's and had a shave – we had breakfast in a café not far from Lyon station. I went through the morning paper to see whether it carried anything about us. Aristide had come up trumps. There was a brief notice of the sinking of the barge and the deaths by drowning of two women and one man – all as yet unidentified. The last paragraph said that the barge captain, Grognon, had disappeared and was wanted for questioning. If Billings and company saw it, then we should have some cover for a while.

By half-past nine we were out on the ring road to the east of Lyon. I stood back and Bertina thumbed us a lift within half a minute. It was a Simca 1000, driven by a young man on his way to Grenoble. He was dark-haired, good-looking, and was returning to the University at Grenoble after spending a weekend at his home in the Auvergne.

In Grenoble I went to the nearest *Bureau de Poste et Télégraphe* to get Dufy's telephone number and check that he was still listed at the address I had been given by Wilkins.

He was listed all right: *Garage Dufy, Meylan, T43.60.93.* A girl behind one of the grilles told me that Meylan was about a couple of kilometres north of Grenoble on the N90, which was the road that ran up to Chambéry and Aix-les-Bains.

I was getting a bit low on my money now. In the back of my wallet I always carried – and I'd had them for about ten years against some emergency – five American twenty-dollar bills. We went into a bank. Long-faced President Jackson looked up at me rather reproachfully as I handed the bills over. We'd been friends for years. But there comes a time when you must sell even your best friend.

We caught a bus out to Meylan, parked our case in a *buvette*, and took a look around. It was less a village than a straight stretch of N90 with a sprawl of buildings along-side it.

The Garage Dufy was a low, white-faced building a few yards back from the road, and with an open space to one side where a choice collection of wrecked cars rusted quietly away in the sun. The big double doors were open and I could see a couple of mechanics sprawled under a car, and beyond them in the back of the garage the dark blue van. Iron steps ran up the yard side of the garage to a small superstructure on the roof which had windows facing the road. On the door was painted the word – *Bureau*.

About a hundred yards away on the other side of the road from the garage, was a tall stretch of railings that needed painting and behind them a tree-shaded spread of untidy grass with a dirt drive that led up to a small château. Along the railings was a huge sign which read – *Hôtel Château de la Revirée*. It looked just about our cup of tea.

I went back to the wine shop, got the case, and then we made for the *Revirée*. I explained that my car had broken down and was in a local garage for repairs and I wanted rooms for myself and my sister for a couple of nights.

That evening, leaving Bertina at the hotel, I checked the Garage Dufy. It closed at nine, but a light showed in the office until nine-thirty. Then the light went out. A man came down the iron steps, got into a car parked in front of the double doors and drove off towards Grenoble. It was Dufy. I gave him fifteen minutes and then I went out of the side gate of the hotel garden and walked down to the garage.

At the back of the garage I found a loo window an inch open on a catch. I flipped the catch bar off, pushed the window back and scrambled in. The loo door gave direct into the garage. I flicked on my torch and had a look round. As I swung it to get my bearings, I saw a keyboard above a work-bench with a row of hooks that had greasy labels above them. One of the hooks was labelled – *Bureau*. I took it.

I went over to the blue van.

It had double doors at the back and one was open. I climbed up and flashed the torch around. There was a canvas sheet folded in one corner, a strawpacked carboy in a wire frame alongside it, and a crumpled copy of *Le Figaro* stuck through one of the side struts. I squatted down in the centre of the floor and rubbed my hands across it. There was a film of cement dust on them.

I went out through the loo window and then up the iron steps to the bureau.

I unlocked the door, slipped in, shut the door and then gave the quickest of flicks of the torch at the windows. Over the top of them was a roller blind. I pulled it down and was showered with dust and dead blue-bottles.

I switched on the light and had a look round. It was the untidiest place ever. There was a big desk that was bulging with papers, bills, and brochures, not to mention odd things like fan belts, piston rings and a litter of sparking plug cartons. There was a kitchen clock on top, ticking away erratically as though it were due for a coronary at any moment. A kitchen chair stood in front of the desk and there was a green filing cabinet against the wall by the window. On a shelf near the door – where it could just not be reached from the desk – was an old-fashioned telephone looking like a dusty, black, deformed daffodil.

I went over to it. The one thing I'd been banking on was that Dufy must have some means of communicating with Billings. The obvious way was by telephone.

On the wall above the telephone was a Total petrol calendar. Alongside it, on the plain deal boarding, was a long list of telephone numbers. The numbers were all written in the same hand. It was a pleasant surprise to see that the last number was Divonne 64. This was the number of the Golf hotel. Among the six numbers above this there were two Grenoble numbers, an Aix-les-Bains number, then three others that meant nothing to me. Billings's hideaway was in the country, so I decided to skip the Grenoble and Aix numbers and concentrate on the others. I rang the first two and got no reply.

The last of the three read – Aiguebelette-le-lac 91.

I asked for this and, while I waited, I considered the prospect of having to tackle Dufy personally. It was something

I didn't want to have to do – so I crossed my fingers. There were quite a few numbers higher up I could still try.

After a small interval of clicks and buzzes, a man's voice said, 'Aiguebelette, quatre-vingt-onze.'

I didn't answer. But I kept my fingers crossed.

The voice said sharply, 'Allo? Ici Aiguebelette, quatre-vingt-onze. Qui est là?'

His accent was almost as bad as mine. I still didn't answer.

The voice went on irritably, 'Allo! Allo! Qui est bloody well là?' Then there was a pause, and in a sudden burst of petulance the voice went on, 'Who's there? Parlez s'il vous – Oh, for God's sake, this damn' phone!' The receiver was slammed down.

I rang off my end, too. The whole thing was pure Hasler, and he seemed in a bad temper about something.

I went out, put the key back in the main garage, and returned to the hotel. At the desk I borrowed a copy of *Le Guide Michelin,* and took it up to Bertina's room.

I said, 'I think I've found the place where they are. At least the telephone number. Hasler answered when I rang.'

'Wasn't that dangerous?'

'No. He just thought it was a wrong call.'

In the Michelin, I found *AIGUEBELETTE* (*Lac d'*). It was a lake about fifty-eight kilometres due north from Grenoble, up in the hills and not far from the Chartreuse massif. Chartreuse rang a bell.

Bertina said, 'So what now?'

I said, 'We're going up there. Billings isn't necessarily going to hang about long in one place.'

'And how do we go?'

I went over to the window and looked out. The garden lights were on and there were three cars parked on the gravel drive outside.

I said, 'I think we'll take the Mercedes. I noticed that the keys were in it as I came by.'

'You're crazy!'

'This is no time to muck about with car hire and having

190

to show passports. You go down and wait for me at the main gate.'

She hesitated.

I said, 'Go on.'

She said, 'What you're doing is mad.'

'Maybe,' I said. 'But I can't think of anything else. I want those diamonds.'

'Just to get me out of trouble? That still makes you crazy. I'm not going to let you do this. Why should you? It's nothing to do with you. I let myself drift into all this – I should have my head examined. But, at least, I've got enough sense now to know that you can't just walk in on Billings and the rest. They'd just put you through the mincer. I'm not worth it.'

I said, 'Don't fuss, duckie. It isn't just for you. I thought it might be a good idea if I just did something for once that I wouldn't mind thinking about in my quiet moments. Now, get down to the main gate. We'll leave all our stuff here.'

The Mercedes was a beautiful car, and I drove it with great respect for the privilege of being allowed to borrow it. It was still dark when we made the lake, and we both took cat naps until the sun came up over the mountains. We drove along the lake side and found a small hotel for breakfast. I borrowed their *Botin* and looked up Aigue-belette 91. It was listed as G. Hibaud. Le Manoir de l'Epine, Saint-Sulpice. The girl who served our breakfast said that Saint-Sulpice was a small village up in the mountains, about four kilometres dead east of the lake. She knew the Manoir, Monsieur Hibaud had not lived in it for more than ten years – he was an industrialist in Lyon. The house was let from time to time to different people. She had no idea who lived there now. The house was reached by a long private drive that led off the main road just before one entered the village of Saint-Sulpice.

We reached the drive entrance just before ten. I turned into it, went about two hundred yards along it and then pulled off across close turf and into some pine trees, well out of sight of the driveway.

I checked my automatic. 'Now listen – you keep out of the way. If anyone shows up, get back into the woods.'

As I got out of the car, she said, 'I still don't want you to do it.'

I grinned. 'You're as bad as Wilkins – but much better looking.'

I headed for the pines, away from the drive.

THIRTEEN

Diamonds are Trumps

THE MANOIR lay in a small bowl of land, rimmed by the surrounding crests of the hills. It was a big house; originally a small château, but over a couple of centuries – various people – clearly not architects – had had fun with it. It was all over the place. If Horace had ever tried to paint it, he would have had hell's own delight with the perspective. At one end was a tall, dome-capped structure which looked like an old observatory. A balcony ran around the base of the dome, and there was an iron ladder down the side of the tower to the ground. In front of the house was a big garden laid out in geometrical patches of gravel and grass. At the other end of the house a great sweep of steps curved down to a driveway. Parked at the foot of the steps was Lian's Lancia and a big Citroen station-wagon.

I worked my way round to the far end of the house, where the woods and scrub ran close in to the gardens, so that I had only about ten yards of open ground to cover to reach the foot of the steel ladder. I waited, watching for any sign of movement from the house, and then made a dash. The ladder had rusted badly in places and some of the supports were loose, so I went up very carefully. On the catwalk I was confronted by a low, narrow doorway let into the curve of the dome. The door was bolted on the outside and it took me some time to ease the bolt back without noise.

It opened inwards and I slipped in. I was on a wooden-floored gallery that ran around the inside of the dome. To my right wooden steps ran down to the floor of the observatory. Down below I could see some armchairs, a covered billiard table and a litter of rolled carpets and packing cases. Dust lay thick over them all. On the far side of the gallery was a small door. I went over to it.

It was half open and I went through to find myself in a narrow corridor whose linoleum was also thick with dust. It was not hard to guess that I was in an unused part of the house.

The corridor ran for about fifty yards and then turned sharp right. As I turned the corner I was met by a blaze of sunlight.

A few feet in front of me was a wrought-iron railing and above it a glass roof that ran backwards for about eighty feet. I went quietly to the railing and recognized the place at once. From a little balcony, close up under the glass roof, I was looking down into the conservatory where I had had my talk with Fairlawn and Billings. A great spray of maidenhair fern, growing from some trough low on the other side of the railing, arched up in front of me. Iron steps led from the balcony down to the floor. From wall pots and beds, exotic plants reached up to the glass roof. In the middle of the tiled floor below was the long water lily tank, and, against the far wall, the tanks for tropical fish ... tiger barbs and cherry barbs ... I was heading right for a fine collection of tiger barbs.

One of them, in fact, was sitting below me. It was Billings. He wore a light-coloured linen suit, black waistcoat and an immaculate white shirt. He was talking on a telephone which stood on a small cane table at his side. His free hand held a cigar.

He was saying, 'Yes, we're leaving in the next hour. And as soon as I get down there, your people have got to be on hand – and ready to buy ... No ...' his voice rose slightly. 'All I can tell you is, I don't want the transaction done here. I've changed my plans.'

Whoever it was on the other end came back with something and Billings sat there, nodded his big head and cuddled the cigar in the corner of his mouth.

'All right,' he said finally. 'We'll be there, about midnight.'

He put the receiver back, and stood up. As he did so I saw that beyond the lily tank were stacked three cement sacks. He was sitting there with his cargo ready for shipment.

Only, if I could do anything about it – it was never going to be shipped, never going to make him a fat profit out of the tragedies of other people.

He strolled slowly over to one of the tanks and stood studying the fish.

At this moment Fairlawn, Hasler and Lian came into the conservatory. Hasler stayed near the doorway, an automatic in his hand.

Lian was in a grey silk suit, with a little straw boater perched on her head which brought back memories to me. Fairlawn, a big, charming smile all over his face, was carrying a slim suitcase which I recognized at once as the one which had held the diamonds when Horace had valued them.

Billings turned and stared ponderously at the three of them. His gaze went slowly from Hasler's automatic to the suitcase in Fairlawn's hand. Of the two he showed, I thought, more surprise over the suitcase. Not that he showed much of anything. It wasn't his style.

Billings said, 'I seem to recognize that case.'

Fairlawn nodded. 'The diamonds,' he said. 'We've still got them.'

For a moment Billings was silent. Then he said, 'And Suma?'

Lian said, 'We left her on the barge with the other two.'

Billings shook his head. 'You are all fools. Honour amongst thieves – it's a cliché. But a good one. And it's the only thing that works.' He raised his hand curtly as Fairlawn started to say something. 'Don't bother. I can see the whole picture. Well, you may have a brief and uneasy happiness, Make what you can of it. This dishonourable

195

act and Suma's death will never be forgotten. The People's Republic will reach out for you.'

Fairlawn said, 'We're all ready to get loaded up. We're leaving the Lancia here and taking the other car. The housekeeper's gone. She won't be back until this evening. Before we leave there are one or two things to clear up.' He flashed Billings a smile full of charm and courtesy.

'It's a polite way of putting it. Thank you.'

I had to admire Billings. He was completely unruffled. But then had he ever been otherwise?

'There's nothing personal in this, of course,' said Fairlawn.

'I would like to think that was so,' said Billings.

Fairlawn shrugged his shoulders. 'Sorry. You know . . . parting of the ways. Life must go on.'

Billings smiled. Clearly he had an ear for irony.

'We do not intend that you go with us.'

It was Lian. I might have known it had to be. Women are always impatient with preliminaries.

Billings gave a little nod. 'I'd already gathered that. You won't forget, of course, that there are a lot of people in London still to be paid. When they're disappointed some of them might get you before the Chinese do.' He then looked direct at Hasler and I knew the bid was coming. 'Hasler,' he said, 'don't join this company of fools. Shoot Fairlawn and you can have his share.'

It was a moment or two before Hasler spoke. Then he said, 'I'm sorry. But you know what would happen. I'd never live to enjoy it. You couldn't ever forgive me.'

Fairlawn smiled, and said, 'Good try. Hasler's right.'

Billings nodded. 'Yes, I'm afraid he is.'

Lian, her voice a little shrill, said, 'Finish with this.'

Fairlawn gave her a loving look and then turned towards Hasler and nodded. Through the maidenhair ferns in front of me, I saw his gun come up without hurry. He should have hurried. In fact they'd been too damned leisurely with the whole thing. If you've got a nasty job to do, do it fast. So I did.

I didn't try any funny stuff like trying to blow his hand off. After all it was Casalis's gun and I wasn't too sure how accurate I could be. I just pumped two shots, fast, at the region of his heart.

He did a backward flip like a marionette gone haywire and lay on the ground. It was damned bad shooting because he moved, yelled, and clutched at his left shoulder. With my own gun he would never have moved.

I stepped out on to the head of the stairs, just as Lian – God, what a woman – began to move towards Hasler's gun that lay on the tiles a yard from him.

'Go on, little cherry blossom,' I said. 'Pick it up and I'll blow your bloody head off.'

She stopped in midflight and slowly straightened. I came down the stairs, all of them watching me, and it was a superb entrance. And when I reached the bottom step I stopped and could have had their attention for that actor's dream – a fifteen-minute speech without a single interruption – except that this was no dream.

Billings said, 'Thank you, Mr Carver.'

I said, 'Anyone speaks – it's me. From now. Anyone moves other than I say and this time I shoot knowing it kicks high and right. So – Fairlawn, you get one end of Hasler, and you, Billings, the other. Lian you stay just where you are and keep your hands above your head.'

It's a wonderful thing power. People do what you say and that makes for happiness. Lian's hands went up and the two men obediently lifted Hasler like a sagging roll of carpet.

I said, 'We'll go down to the cellar where Horace did the valuation. Men first, then Lian.'

They began to move out of the door, and I motioned Lian to fall in behind them.

I went out, close behind them and I was hoping that my memory of the door to the cellar was accurate, a big steel door with bolts on the outside.

Crossing the big hall where Bertina had given me coffee

Fairlawn, who was just in front of Lian, turned his head back and said, 'Look, Carver, old—'

I fired and took a chunk out of the parquet floor six inches from his feet. His head swung back and, believe it or not, up ahead I heard Billings give one of his imperial chuckles.

At the end of the corridor, the basement steps dropped sharply downwards. The men carried Hasler down awkwardly, and I crowded close up behind Lian, her arms still in the air. The door below was half open and I could see the bolts on it. In addition, which I hadn't remembered, there was a lock with a key.

Billings squeezed through the partly open door and the rest followed. I stood at the door and watched. They carried Hasler to the long table and put him on it. He'd passed out with pain and just lay there. They all three turned and faced me.

I said, 'I don't think you'll have to wait long. I'm phoning for the police.' I gave Fairlawn a warm smile, and said, 'It's a great effort, old man, to resist the temptation to pump some lead into you – except it would be a damned bad show. Unarmed man and all that.'

'Don't be squeamish,' said Billings pleasantly. 'Just do me the favour. I suppose the ambitious fool made some stupid mistake on the barge?'

'He was careless with knives. If you stick one in somebody's back you shouldn't leave it there.'

Lian called angrily at Fairlawn, 'Go for him! Go now!'

I saw Fairlawn's right hand dropping for his pocket. I was tempted, really tempted because it would have been so easy. But I resisted it. Barnes would have more fun with him, and he'd have years to brood over it in prison afterwards. I swung the door fast. His shot hit the steel face as it closed and I heard the bullet ricochet like a mad bee around the basement.

I pushed the bolts over at top and bottom, and then turned the key in the lock.

I went back up the steps with a song in my heart. Back

in the conservatory there were several things I had to do. First I checked that the diamonds were in the slim suitcase. They were, but no longer in the mass of little envelopes which had previously held them. They were in three quite big chamois leather pouches. The diamonds checked, I reached for the phone and put through a *Rouge-sous-rouge* call.

It took longer than usual this time. In the end I got Casalis, his voice coming to me through a lot of static. I guessed he was on a radio telephone somewhere.

He said, 'You'll be glad to know we're keeping a cell warm for you, you trouser-stealing bastard.'

I said, 'The boys you want are in the cellar of a house called Le Manoir de l'Epine. That's near Saint-Sulpice, about sixty kilometres north of Grenoble. Be careful how you go in – Fairlawn has a gun. Oh, yes – and have an ambulance come as well.'

'And where shall we find you?'

'I'll be around. But first of all I'm going to give myself a treat. I'm going to take a drive in a Lancia Flavia. Always wanted to.'

'With the girl – Bertina?'

'No. I shall be alone. I've lent her my Mercedes.'

I rang off.

It was a beautiful car, and I treated it with respect over the length of bumpy driveway. When I reached the place where the Mercedes was parked I stopped and got out. I blew the horn and after a moment or two Bertina came out of the pines.

She came fast across to me and made a grab at my arms.

'What happened?'

'Nothing. It's what's going to happen that is important. All I want you to do is to sit in the Mercedes until I get back. No need to do any hiding now.'

'Where are you going? Damn it, why can't you explain things?'

I got back into the Lancia and tapped the slim suitcase

on the seat alongside me. 'I just want to get rid of this. I'll be about an hour.'

'What do you mean – get rid of it? What's in it?'

'You're a one for questions, aren't you? Just sit in the car and wait.'

I moved off and in the rear mirror saw her standing there, watching.

On the main road I put my foot down and she went up to seventy-five mph like a bird and then was hitting ninety before I was ready for it.

I was away for nearly an hour. I guessed that might be the right interval. Coming back up the driveway I saw the Mercedes out on the road. Bertina was sitting in it and Casalis standing alongside.

I drew up.

'All right, Robin Hood,' said Casalis. 'Just drive on to the house ahead of us.'

'Are the others up there?'

'Sure. Sutcliffe, Barnes ... the whole boiling.'

'Quick work.'

'We had this area figured one way and another. Chiefly because of that Lancia you're driving. When you spoke to me it came over the radio telephone. We were between here and Chambéry. Get going.'

I moved on.

In front of the house were three police cars, an ambulance, and a couple of police motor cyclists. Sitting in the back of one of the cars, handcuffed together were Fairlawn and Lian. Fairlawn stared straight through me. Lian turned her head a little to take in Bertina at my side, and then gave a little fatalistic shrug of her shoulders.

The welcoming committee was assembled for us in the conservatory. Billings, handcuffed, was sitting on the cane chair. Aristide, tieless, brown suit ruffled, sleepy eyes blinking, stood behind him. Sutcliffe was over by the fish-tanks, feet planted solidly on the tiles, and was slowly filling a pipe. Seated on another chair was Barnes, jacket off, and a French policeman was giving him first aid on his arm. I could guess what had happened. Despite my warning, old death-and-glory Barnes had gone charging first into the cellar, gun blazing, and had copped one. It would make a good chapter in his memoirs.

When he saw us come in he stood up and brushed the policeman away, flaying a fat hand at him so that the man backed out of the place.

'So,' he bellowed, 'you've come back. That's a surprise.'

'I told Casalis I was coming back,' I said.

He kept coming at me, but only got as far as the pile of cement sacks before Sutcliffe stopped him.

'All right, Barnes,' he said sharply. 'I know this man. Let me handle it.'

'I can handle him,' said Barnes angrily. 'For God's sake, his kind come two a penny.' He swung round on Billings. 'When he shut you up in the cellar, you left the diamonds up here in a suitcase, didn't you?'

'What diamonds?' said Billings, blandly. It was a good ploy, but it wouldn't last long, and he knew it.

As Barnes seethed, Sutcliffe said quietly, 'Commander – you're beginning at the wrong end.'

But there was no stopping him. He had the bit between his teeth. He'd got everything he wanted, except the diamonds, and he meant to have those. Well, he could, at a price. He swung on Bertina and roared, 'You saw him drive off. Did he have a suitcase with him?'

Bertina hesitated for a moment and then she said, 'I really didn't see.'

The lid came off the volcano then.

'Don't give me that! You're in deep trouble already. Start any more lies and it will just make it worse.'

'You're talking nonsense,' I said.

Barnes exploded. He came right up to me, red-haired and bulky, a moving volcano, and any moment I expected to see sulphur clouds coming from his ears.

'Don't try that kind of stuff, Carver!'

He lifted his big hands and made a strangler's movement.

I said, 'You come an inch nearer, and I'm going to ask for police protection.'

'You give me any more lip – and I'll tear your head off!'

'Good – then you can mount it on an ebony block and put in on your mantelshelf.'

He took a deep breath, not for control, but to work up a maximum explosive force.

It was then that Sutcliffe stepped in.

He said, 'Commander Barnes – leave this to me!' The words went through the place like an arctic wind. As Barnes looked at him, frozen for a moment by the icy blast, Sutcliffe went on to me, 'All right, Carver. Let's have it. Just the essentials.'

I said contritely, 'You asked me to work for you, and I did to the best of my ability. I was double-crossed over the diamond-drug exchange point. For a while there it was a little rough, for Bertina and myself. And let's get this straight – she had no part in the diamond stealing. Isn't that right?' I looked at Billings. He just smiled, but it was sympathetically.

'Why make that point?' asked Sutcliffe.

'Because some people think otherwise. I don't like to see the innocent suffer.'

Barnes gave a sudden rumble in his throat and said, 'Ah, now I see what you're after. You won't get away with that. I'm not making any deal.'

I said, 'It's going to take some of the shine off your glory having a trial with the diamonds still not recovered.'

'You've hidden them?'

'Of course he has,' said Sutcliffe impatiently. 'Why the hell do you think he called Casalis and then drove away from here?'

'I'll run a small tooth comb through this countryside!'

'Do that,' I said. 'And get out the frogmen for the lakes and ponds, and chaps with pitchforks for the haystacks.

Some men with spades would be helpful too.'

I lit a cigarette and I could see that he took it as a personal insult.

'The girl's an accomplice – clearly established,' snorted Barnes. I had a feeling he was just restraining himself from pawing the ground like a challenging stallion. 'Nobody's altering that fact.'

'You'll have to find a way – if you want the diamonds. Of course, if you don't care about them—'

'You're under arrest,' he said.

'Okay,' I said, 'then I'd like to see my lawyer before I say any more.' I strolled over to one of the fish tanks and watched a couple of young fantail goldfish idling around showing off their finery.

Sutcliffe said, 'This man works for me. As such he enjoys some special privileges. I don't want him arrested.'

'Why the hell not?' Barnes glanced at him.

I turned and said, 'When I arrived the people here were on the point of leaving. I stopped that. You've got them, you've got the drugs – and you can have the diamonds. At a price.'

'No dealing,' said Barnes. 'We'll find them.'

'I don't think you will.' I moved back towards Barnes. 'Why don't you be sensible? The girl means nothing to you – you've got the others. And you could have the diamonds. Anyway – there it is. You choose.'

'I'll see you in hell first! You can't blackmail the police!'

'It's been done,' I said.

'Carver!'

It was Sutcliffe – and I got the icy blast.

I said, 'Make him see sense then.'

It was at this moment that Billings spoke. He had his fat handcuffed hands resting on his waistcoat, as he sat comfortably settled in his cane chair.

'May I say ...' he hesitated, waiting for attention; '... that it is nice to see this young man so determined. Romantic, chivalrous. Two qualities that have always appealed to me. However, that is not the point. I would

203

just like to say that to the best of my knowledge and belief Bertina never knew anything about the plan to steal diamonds—'

'But you admit you did!' Barnes said.

'Well, naturally. I planned it. But she knew nothing. I thought – since I'm now bored with the whole business – that this was a good moment to make that crystal clear.'

As he finished speaking he raised his handcuffed hands to his mouth. I saw Aristide jump forward and grab for his arms. But he was too late. Billings clamped his mouth shut. Five seconds later his body gave a horrible twitch and collapsed to the floor.

'Poison!'

It was Barnes shouting the obvious.

Sutcliffe, unmoved – in his world it was a common thing for men to walk around with self-destruction tablets in their waistcoat pockets – got up and went over to Barnes.

He put a hand on his elbow and said, 'I'd like a word with you in private.'

Barnes, shaken by Billings's death – it had taken the star prisoner from his trial – let himself be led out of the room.

Aristide went out and brought back a couple of men to move Billings. Bertina came over to me and I put an arm round her shoulder.

'What's going to happen?' she said.

I shrugged my shoulders.

'Anyone's bet,' said Casalis.

My arm still round her shoulder, I crossed my fingers. In one of the fish tanks a golden orfe swam to the glass front and took a look at us. What he saw bored him and he turned away.

Time marched by on leaden feet. Then I realized that it was my heart thumping. Time still passed. My crossed fingers grew sticky with sweat.

Fifteen minutes later Barnes and Sutcliffe came back. Sutcliffe came up to me.

'The Commander and I have gone into this thing, Carver. Very generously, in view of the services which you and this young lady have rendered, he's decided to guarantee her complete immunity. If you want it in writing you can have it.'

I looked at Barnes. I could feel Bertina close against me, one of her hands holding the slack of my jacket sleeve.

'No,' I said. 'His word is good enough for me.' I walked away up the row of fish tanks. The end one had been cleaned out and stood full of water, ready for restocking.

I said, 'You won't have to go digging around the countryside for the diamonds. They're in here.'

They were, scattered across the bottom, making a pleasant new gravelly bed to the tank. All that was needed were a few rocks and weeds and a handful of tiger and cherry barbs to make it worthy of the Ascanti Club.

We drove back across France leisurely in the Ford. There was no point in hurrying. After Le Touquet there was only London ahead ... that meant being jammed up again on the Central Line, cracked cups in cafés, dirty shirt cuffs, and Mrs Meld banging about in the morning giving out with *Drink to me Only*, slamming the bedroom door open and shouting, 'Morning, Mr Carver. How many eggs and how do you want 'em done?'

Mornings should be peaceful. Like this one. We hadn't been able to get into Le Manoir hotel at Le Touquet, so we'd taken a chalet in the motel alongside. Very peaceful.

I looked down at the pillow at my side. Bertina's blonde hair was all over it. She was sleeping like a tired child. The black silk nightdress had slipped clear from her beautiful shoulders.

I got out of bed carefully to avoid waking her and went into the tiny kitchen to fix coffee and eggs and I felt good. And I liked that. Coffee, I told myself, and four eggs, two with their eyes open, and two fried both sides.

Victor Canning

Acclaimed as 'one of the six finest thriller writers in the world'.

QUEEN'S PAWN 30p

'Beautifully engineered plot, hair-trigger suspense, set-piece climactic excitements aboard *QE2*: typically compulsive Canning' – THE SCOTSMAN

THE SCORPIO LETTERS 30p

'Canning spins an ingenious plot, and manoeuvres his cosmopolitan cast across half Europe with never a dull moment – THE IRISH TIMES

'Crisp thriller . . . the mysterious blackmailer Scorpio is excitingly and violently unmasked' – DAILY EXPRESS

THE WHIP HAND 30p

'An excellent book for any spy fans . . . Canning plays out another tense, fast-moving tale. Rex Carver, private detective, follows a beautiful girl from Brighton to the Continent and into a spider's web of danger and intrigue' – EVENING STANDARD

THE MELTING MAN 30p

'Few more macabre settings for a climax could be imagined than the private waxworks of a mountain chateau . . . Crisp, polished and as tense as they come' – BRISTOL EVENING NEWS

Gavin Lyall

'A complete master of the suspense technique'
— LIVERPOOL DAILY POST

THE MOST DANGEROUS GAME   30p

'Superior suspense . . . excellent flying details'
— THE OBSERVER

SHOOTING SCRIPT   30p

'The sky's the limit for this fine suspense/
adventure story'   — DAILY MIRROR

MIDNIGHT PLUS ONE   30p

'Grimly exciting . . . original in concept, ex-
pertly written and absolutely hair-raising'
— NEW YORK TIMES

THE WRONG SIDE OF THE SKY   30p

'One of the year's best thrillers'
— DAILY HERALD

VENUS WITH PISTOL   30p

'Thrillers on this level are rare enough'
— DAILY TELEGRAPH

Dick Francis